BEYOND THE DOORS

BEYOND
THE
DOORS

Clay Kelly

Illustrations and cover art by Christa M. Kelly

Pygmy Possum Press
claykellywrites@gmail.com
www.claykellywrites.con

ISBN 978 1838340 605

British Library Cataloguing in Publication Data.
A catalogue record for this book is available from the British Library.

Printed and bound in Great Britain by 4edge Limited
Illustrations and cover art by Christa M. Kelly

For Hazel

ONE

In the last moments before her world split apart, Hazel slipped into the shadows under the stairs, shivering in the damp night air. She hadn't been alone since she joined hundreds of other children marching up the gangplank of the *SS Minerva*, bound for Halifax. In fact, since the day her parents sat across from her – awkwardly formal in the good chairs usually reserved for company – there had been little time to think about what was happening. A Nazi invasion of England was probable, and Hazel was being evacuated to Canada. Alone.

As the dark night over the Atlantic thickened around her, Hazel thought again of that conversation with her parents. Their faces bore a look she had known for as long as she could remember; a look reserved only for her. They stared at her as though they didn't know her, as though they were surprised to find her in their house. Among her quiet, respectable, country family, Hazel was like a fish out of water. And so, despite the frightening circumstances, Hazel's heart had lifted at the prospect of visiting a wide world in which she might find a place to fit in. She loved her family but hoped – believed – there was more.

Hazel made her way to the rail and looked back towards England. Not even the faintest outline of the coast remained. Somewhere back there, her homeland was under attack. Bombs were dropping on London and the whole country. Everyone had a relation or friend off at war; too many lives were being lost. Yet here she was, the steady crash of waves putting miles between herself and the conflict in Europe. Hazel had no idea how to feel.

She peered through the darkness toward the other ships which made up their convoy. She could just make them out, grey against the black sea – and the ghostly companions gave her comfort. Hazel's parents hadn't spoken of it, but the children at the dock were abuzz with rumours of lost transport ships, sunk by Nazi torpedoes from submarines deep in the ocean. Thinking of being hunted from below made her shudder.

A loud shout from above shook Hazel from her thoughts and she slid back under the stairs.

"Where are you, lad? I know yer here somewhere!" a man's voice called.

"Have you lost the little rat?" asked another voice. "Not a few hours out to sea and the boat is crawling with filthy rats."

"Take it easy, Trevor, chasing scabby kids around the deck beats sitting in a hole in France waiting for Nazi bullets," the first voice responded with a snort.

As the voices began to move away, Hazel saw a boy about her age turn the corner. Though the night was dark, she had the oddest sense that he was bathed in moonlight. She gasped when he turned his head and looked right into her eyes – as if he could clearly see her – despite the shadows. He took one look around and dove in next to her.

"Ow!" she cried when he trod on her foot.

"Pardon me," said the boy. "I hope it's all right if I join you, best hiding place on the deck and you found it first." The footsteps grew louder again; he pushed in closer to Hazel and they saw the passing forms of two navy-blue-coated figures.

A voice called from the deck above, "Hey Trevor, head to the mess. I hear Cook's got something nice on the hob. Not strictly speaking regulation, if you catch my meaning."

Trevor apparently liked the idea since his footfall moved on in the other direction once again.

"Well, I don't know about you," whispered the boy with a sigh, "but I'm not certain I feel safe in the hands of those fine gents!" He stood up, brushed off his trousers and offered his hand. "I'm Bec."

"Bec?" asked Hazel getting to her own feet. "Odd name." She immediately dropped her head, shaking it slightly; just the sort of awkward comment her mother always chided her for.

"I suppose I am an odd fellow," he responded. His face wore a crooked smile.

"I'm Hazel. Not odd," she added. "I'm sorry I was rude."

"Miss Hazel Notodd. An extraordinary name, actually," said Bec, his brown eyes twinkling in a pleasant manner. Even in the dimness of the hiding place, Bec still seemed to glow a little so Hazel's heart nearly stopped when he said, "You shine a bit, if you don't mind me saying." His face turned a bright shade of red as he said it and Hazel matched it with an equally bright blush. "I mean sort of like there's lightning in you."

"I, uh…" Hazel stammered. "I mean you… uh… I mean to say…" She tried to find the right words, but she had as little experience talking to boys as she did talking about glowing people. "You do too!" she finally spat out.

"Do I?" responded Bec, his smile broadening. "How delightful! Though not very helpful for sneaking about the deck. Must be something to do with the mist and the sea air, don't you think? I have a climatology book in the cabin, I shall look it up!" he said with a contented nod, seeming satisfied that the mystery had been cleared up.

Hazel raised her eyebrows but her lips involuntarily turned up in a smile and she had the unique sensation of feeling comfortable with a stranger.

"It's actually Francis Xavier Dolman Beckwith," the boy said, looking a bit sheepish.

"Really?" she asked with a little laugh. "That's a lot."

"Sadly, yes. 'You are to inherit a great title and property Francis and you must compost yourself appropriately at all times'," Bec quoted with his chin in the air – speaking as if his nose was bunged up.

"Um, do you maybe mean comport?" Hazel suggested with a giggle.

"You're quite right. Yes, that would certainly make more sense, wouldn't it? Well I'm thinking my father would not think much of my comportment just now. Scurrying about on deck at night, intruding on the privacy of a lady. I suppose I'm lucky that he's a few hundred miles away already."

"Sounds like evacuation to Canada might be to your liking?" asked Hazel.

Bec swished his lips back and forth as if trying to taste his answer; then he nodded. "I'm thinking it might work out well. They decided to send me off quickly enough, but it took me ages to convince my parents to let me get placed with a family in Canada like everyone else. Father had in mind to send me to stay with Lord Tredbarren's cousin in New York but some days I think he dislikes Americans more than the Nazis! In the end, Father was torn between all the manly character I might build in Canada and fear that I will lose my breeding in the hands of some colonial savage. Anyhow, I'm on board and safe from the bonds of being a Beckwith."

Hazel gave the boy a slight smile but had no idea what to say.

"Bonds of being a Beckwith," Bec repeated, "try saying that ten times quickly." Hazel shrugged and repeated the line over and over until it sounded like the clucking of chickens in the yard. They both had to stop for laughing. Hazel felt layers of tension and loneliness peel away.

Bec took a breath and looked at Hazel, "What about you? You don't seem like you are up here on deck weeping with homesickness – if you don't mind me saying."

"It's all right. I suppose I am a bit relieved to get away. I've barely been away from home, you see, and it feels like maybe an adventure would be good. Some independence."

"What about your friends? Are there any on the ship?" Bec asked shyly.

Hazel knew she could fib; this boy would never know the difference, but somehow she didn't feel like lying to him. "I don't really have any," she said looking down. "Mum schooled me at home; she needed my help on the farm, you see. Well, I just never really had the chance to make any."

"Quite understandable. I had a series of stuffy tutors at home. Rather the same situation," Bec said with a pleasant smile that made Hazel's unease slip away.

"What are you doing up here on deck?" Hazel asked.

"Ah, well," Bec began, "the lads in my cabin were not very kind about my book collection. You would think there is something wrong with keeping some basic reference materials on hand. The damp deck seemed less unpleasant than staying with those lugs."

"Sorry to hear that," Hazel replied. "Boys can be so rude! I mean, *you* aren't, but many are… Well, you know…" She flushed at yet another awkward comment. *What on earth was she doing expressing an opinion about boys in general*, she thought. *As if she knew any!*

"Developmental stage, actually," Bec said matter-of-factly. "People our age experience all manner of hormonal and physiological changes, I've read. All very normal. Not all very fun." It was Bec's turn to flush. "Blast it. Saying just that sort of thing got me into the bind with the lads in the first place."

"No, it's interesting!" Hazel assured the boy – though she wasn't sure what all the words meant.

Bec smiled his appreciation and then asked, "Are you on your own, only child like me?"

"Actually, two sisters and a brother. But I'm the only one they sent away." She saw Bec raise an eyebrow and continued, "My oldest sister, Janet, is a nurse and works in a hospital in London. Dahlia was sent to Aunt Emily in Scotland, near Inverness. Aunt Emily wanted company in case a German parachute landed in the village, but not 'too much company'. She meant me. Baby Ned is staying with Mummy as he's too small to do anything else."

Bec smiled sympathetically. "It's soggy in Scotland anyhow. Do you miss them?"

"I suppose…" Hazel began, thinking about how little time she ever really spent with her sisters, who made it clear they found her odd. They mocked her imaginative questions and teased her about her careless appearance. Hazel had always supposed that was just how siblings were, but she longed to be accepted despite her quirks.

Hazel gave a small smile and said, "Well, baby Ned is lovely; so round he might bounce. I wish he could have come with me."

Their attention was drawn by a dull hum from behind the ship. Hazel moved to the rail with Bec following behind. Turning back toward the distant coast, her ears pricked up and strained to make out the sound. It grew steadily louder and the seas slowly began to swell.

"Hazel?" Bec said, his voice a high-pitched squeak. Hazel gripped the rail as the ship began to toss in the rising waves. The hum grew into a dull roar which grew ever closer. Hazel's mind flipped quickly between options: A Luftwaffe air strike, an explosion from a ship, a tidal wave. Each one made her heart pound in her chest.

"Where is everyone?" Hazel shouted. No one had appeared from belowdecks and none of the other ships seemed to come alive as the unknown threat grew closer.

"I don't like this!" Bec called in reply.

"Should we warn someone?" Her head turned all around to see where she might go to alert the crew, but her hands stayed clenched around the railing.

Then they saw it. As the angry sea tossed the convoy, a flash of lightning crashed down from above. At least it seemed like lightning. Rather than a bolt that flashed and then dispersed, the lightning tore open the sky ripping it from top to bottom like a zipper – just off the side of their ship. There, in the torn space they could clearly see the skyline of a city: tall buildings set against a blue, midday sky.

Hazel shrieked and threw up a hand to shade her eyes from the searing white light. Her other fist remained clasped to the rail – knuckles white as bone. She saw Bec fall back onto the slick deck and try to propel himself away from the rail. Strangely, Hazel's fear was paired with a warmth that charged through her body, almost drawing her toward the opening in the sky. Through the light, she saw a beautiful shimmering silver form flit amongst the buildings in the view beyond, both angelic and frightening at once. Her free hand rose up, almost against her will, and stretched toward the light.

"Hazel, no!" cried Bec.

The panicked shout distracted her momentarily; she turned to look at the boy on the deck and then back to the rift in the sky. The electric tear remained but the form vanished and the cityscape beyond began to waiver and fade. Finally, the opening seemed to mend itself leaving nothing behind but an inky sky and a few twinkling stars. The ship and the sea were calm.

Hazel drew a faltering breath and sank to the deck next to Bec.

"W-w-hat?" he stuttered in response.

"Was that?" continued Hazel, finishing his question.

Bec drew a deep breath and reasoned, "We're under a great deal of strain, aren't we? We're on a ship in wartime, moving to a distant country to live with strangers. We're likely having paranoid delusions, right?"

"The same delusion?" she asked.

"Oh, dear. Not likely," Bec replied, his breath ragged.

"Or maybe it's the sea air, like you said," she added, unconvincingly.

Bec nodded and was about to share an additional hypothesis when he was interrupted.

"Oy, you there," came a cry from above.

"Scatter!" yelped Bec and they scrambled to their feet and ran off in different directions.

TWO

The days were long and grey. Many of the children were seasick, curled in their bunks or huddled on deck. As she had never been to sea, Hazel was surprised to find herself feeling fine. She kept to herself; sometimes reading, but mostly standing at the rails looking out at the other ships of the convoy and thinking about the rift. The boys and girls rarely mixed and Hazel and Bec stayed apart – neither keen to draw attention.

At night, however, Hazel slipped away from the cramped cabin and sat under the stairs with Bec. They hadn't talked the day after the rift, but she somehow knew he would be back under the stairs all the same. He brought biscuits his nanny had sent in his suitcase and they sat, ate and talked. They talked about what they saw until their throats were raw and their eyes itched with lack of sleep. Still, they had no answers.

"You still shimmer, you know," Bec said one night, looking at her with his head cocked to one side. "Hasn't anyone ever noticed before?"

"Just you," Hazel replied. "No one ever really notices me. I'm about as ordinary as they come. I mean until I started sharing delusions with you, that is. What about you?"

"You're the only one to mention it. Think something is wrong with us? Fungal infection maybe, affecting our brains and skin?" Bec held his arm up to the light and tried to detect anything unusual about his skin.

Hazel gave a rueful laugh. "I can't think of a time when I wasn't wondering what's wrong with me."

He smiled sympathetically and handed Hazel another one of the nanny's mouth-watering ginger biscuits.

"Nana Lila is convinced I'll starve in Canada. I tried to tell her they have more food there without a war on their doorstep, but she's obsessed with starvation, mostly mine."

"She sounds nice," Hazel responded through a mouthful of biscuit, spraying crumbs as she spoke. She liked that Bec smiled a bit at the corner of his mouth, but he didn't laugh or tease her.

"She's the best," Bec responded. "She pretty much brought me up. Stupid, weepy story of a rich kid whose parents don't pay attention to him. I sound like such a baby, what with all the suffering going on around us!"

"There's more than one reason to be sad," Hazel said.

After a long, quiet moment, Bec changed the subject and asked, "Where do you think we'll be placed? Canada is enormous. Lila and I looked at Father's atlas; it's about one hundred Englands. There are lots of provinces and England could fit into almost any one of them. It's wider than the ocean we're crossing!"

"Too many facts!" Hazel laughed – then turned to stare out over the dark expanse of ocean.

Bec followed her gaze and sighed. "It would be rather nice if we were near each other. I mean, you know, just to know someone in Canada."

Hazel nodded but could find nothing to say. There really wasn't any chance of them being located near one another and she could already feel an ache growing inside from losing her first real friend. They sat silently for a long while, watching the moonlight dance on the water and the other ships cutting through the black sea.

"Do you think the Nazis will win?" Bec asked after a time.

Hazel smiled but continued seriously. "I don't think the Nazis will take over England. There are too many people fighting back. But I guess I also can't imagine that Germany is filled with bad people either. Don't you think German kids are being sent away from our bombs too?" She felt dreadfully treacherous even suggesting that, but wasn't there always another side to every story?

"There's always another side to a story, isn't there?" asked Bec, as if reading her thoughts.

Hazel's face broke into a smile. Then, unable to explain why, she stood up and began to pace back and forth across the deck. Her mind swept back to their bizarre experience and she pressed on her stomach where a tense knot had begun to form.

"Do you think what we saw has something to do with our glowing thing? I felt a pull toward it – some sort of connection when we saw into that city. I mean, did we make that happen?" There was something absurd about the idea that awkward 'nobody' Hazel could have made something so bizarre and spectacular occur, but she had a nagging itch in her brain that said that the two mysteries were unlikely to have happened by chance.

"I don't know. I just don't know. I mean I guess that would make sense. But I can't even begin to guess what it could be. Maybe something electromagnetic? Physics was never my absolute best subject. I'm unmatched in Latin though," Bec said. "*In qua rapa quod emisti.*"

"Impressive! What does it mean?" Hazel asked.

"Um, where did you buy that turnip? I think," Bec smirked.

Laughing again, Hazel said, "I'll miss you," surprising herself by being so direct. Then she turned from the rail to head back to the cabin. The horizon was turning from black to lilac and she knew she had best be in her bed when the ship was roused for the day.

It was drizzling in Halifax as the ship docked. In the damp and foggy morning Hazel was a little disappointed at how much this distant Canadian port looked like Southampton, from whence they had set sail a week before. The children marched single-file down the clanging gangplank onto the dock. One by one a relief worker checked their identification tags and herded them into a series of queues. They bumped and pushed their way through roped areas and as they were moved into a large pen with a sign that read 'Toronto', Hazel saw Bec.

"We're both in the Toronto group," remarked Bec with a smile when they reached each other.

Just then a grey-faced lady blew a sharp whistle and shouted, "Toronto train leaving. Toronto group follow me." She marched off through the shed and along rain-slicked streets, weaving between warehouses until they saw a train station ahead.

After the tiring walk, lugging their cases from port to station, Hazel and Bec settled into the last seats in the railway carriage and began to read a book together. Bec had a copy of *10,000 Leagues Under the Sea* by Jules Verne with him on the *Minerva* but admitted that he hadn't liked to think about what might be going on under the waves while they were still on the ship.

"Would you like to have an adventure like this?" Bec asked as they finished another chapter.

"Like what? With monsters?" Hazel responded.

"Well, maybe. I just mean a real adventure with danger and high stakes; not just wondering whether they make a good shepherd's pie in Toronto!" Bec answered.

"I'm not sure. On the one hand the world seems quite scary enough without giant squids or fearsome creatures, doesn't it?" Hazel said, thinking of the rift in the dark sky over the ocean and the war they had left behind. "On the other hand, I would rather like to do something big, something real. Being sent away feels so helpless. Maybe thirteen-year-olds aren't meant to save the world, though. Maybe when I'm older," she mused.

Bec nudged her with his shoulder and said, "I wouldn't be so sure. You know, Cleopatra was only ten when she became queen of Egypt."

"Yeah, but she had to marry her brother!" Hazel laughed.

Before they could settle back into reading, four boys from the ship moved into the seats across the aisle from them. They had a newspaper which they spread between them.

"You see this headline?" one boy asked his companions.

They all leaned in and he read aloud. "Squadron of eleven planes disappears over Belgium."

"What in the blazes do they mean 'disappeared'?" asked a deep-voiced boy.

Bec and Hazel pretended to look at their book, but their ears strained to hear the boys' conversation.

"The cover says only that eleven planes out of a twelve-plane squadron just vanished out of the sky," the first one continued.

"Do you mean they were shot down?" asked a little boy.

"Nah, just disappeared. The twelfth pilot was having engine trouble and was lagging behind. He reported that the sky sort of opened up and the other planes just disappeared. Vanished. He's probably a nutter. Shell shock or something."

"Yeah, but the planes are gone, right? Do you think the Nazis have a new weapon? A Vaporiser or something?" questioned the little boy.

"Don't be an idiot, Ian, that's just in Flash Gordon," said the other, but his voice sounded uncomfortable.

"What does the article say, Nigel?" another added impatiently.

It seemed to Hazel rather bad manners to complain when someone was willing to take them in, but she was also a little relieved she hadn't been placed with the vicar, who hadn't offered a smile as yet.

Glancing around, Hazel realised that she was the last one in the station; the matron was collecting her bags and lists and readying to leave.

"Pardon, Miss," whispered Hazel, as she approached the stern woman.

"What is it?" the matron snapped, looking pinched and tired. "Why are you still here?"

Hazel frowned, wondering how exactly her being here – alone in Union Station Toronto – could possibly be her own fault.

Just then, a large, luxurious Rolls-Royce pulled up alongside the curb outside the station, just across from where Hazel stood. A very neat man with jet-black hair, wearing a jade-coloured silk waistcoat and a bowler hat got out of the driver's seat and approached.

"I am here to retrieve the children for Mrs. Withersnips," he said in a formal manner as he pulled a silver-rimmed monocle from his waistcoat and placed it over his eye.

"Well yes, certainly," the matron replied looking a little confused. "This is Hazel Benedict," she gestured to Hazel who smiled and moved forward. The man gave Hazel a long look and removed the monocle. Though she felt slightly uncomfortable, she saw something approving in his eyes that made her feel welcome.

"And the other?" enquired the man.

"Only Hazel. All the others have been retrieved. The

placements are complete," she replied, nervously tapping the pages on her clipboard with a bony finger.

At this, the man's narrow eyes grew worryingly large while his mouth tightened to a thin slash across his face.

"There are meant to be two. There must certainly be two." He held out his hand to the matron who reluctantly handed him her clipboard. He reviewed the pages and then looked around the station, his brow creased in concern. Before the matron could respond, Camilla moved in next to them; clearly, she had detained the vicar and overheard the entire exchange. She stepped in front of the man and blocked his passage.

"I am Camilla Fentermore. I am quite convinced that I am meant to accompany you," she declared with an appraising look at the Rolls-Royce. "I've been assigned to these," she seemed to search for an acceptable word, "... good people in error. I am certain Mrs. Withersnips keeps a more appropriate home and I understand you were expecting another evacuee."

Hazel's heart pounded in her chest though she wasn't certain why. She couldn't tell if she was worried Camilla might come with them or whether she feared they'd swap her place. She found herself inexplicably keen to go with the man in the bowler hat.

The man placed Hazel's case lightly on the floor and removed the monocle from his waistcoat pocket again. He placed it over one dark eye and leaned forward to peer at Camilla. He then removed the monocle, put it back in his pocket, and retrieved the case. He turned to Camilla and said, "Decidedly, no." To Hazel he said, "Wait here." And with that he walked away towards the car, leaving a gaping, red-faced Camilla and the stunned vicar behind.

Outside the station, Hazel saw the man peering up and down the street, monocle pressed to his eye once again, and then hurry out of view with a quick, neat step. When he returned five minutes later, he was carrying a large suitcase and was followed closely by Bec!

THREE

In the hustle and bustle of paperwork that followed, Hazel and Bec could only gape at one another, too confused and delighted to speak. At last, they found themselves tucked into the deep leather backseat of the man's Rolls-Royce. Hazel reached across the seat, took Bec's hand and gave it a squeeze.

"I can't believe it! We're both here and this is…" she breathed in and slumped further into the seat, "… lovely!" As the car pulled out of the station Hazel asked, "But what happened?"

Bec ran his hands through his hair and rubbed his face a few times before he said, "You know, I really don't know. I went away with Miss Crawley, who seemed nice enough – a teacher in a place called Orillia. Had me a bit worried when she said she was a vegetonian or something. Ever heard of one of those? A sort of religion maybe?"

Hazel shook her head and he carried on, "Well, we got to her car and she scampered off for, um, private matters, and left me there on the pavement. Then this gentleman approached," he continued, gesturing to the man in the driver's seat, "and he said I was meant to be placed with him. When Miss Crawley came back, he spoke a few words to her, she nodded to me and drove off. Just like that. She didn't put up much of a fight!"

Hazel and Bec exchanged uncertain glances at the curious, silent man in the front seat. Hazel, deciding to be bold, finally spoke up. "Pardon me, sir, but are we to live with you?"

The man did not hesitate to answer in his undefinable accent, "You will reside at my associate Mrs. Withersnips's house. I am Yi Ju-Long. You may call me Mr. Yi."

"Hello," Hazel responded. "I'm Hazel and this is Bec. Oh dear," she added quietly, "you must already know that."

"I do," Mr. Yi responded. "We have been waiting for you for quite a long time."

There was something ominous in his response that rendered both the children silent – despite the host of questions dancing in each of their minds. Their arrival in Toronto hadn't been delayed, nor had their ship to Halifax, so what could Mr. Yi have meant when he said they had been waiting? Each equally confused, but too nervous to ask, they turned their gazes to the passing scenery, lost in their own reflections.

The light began to grow dim as Hazel watched endless trees pass until her eyelids grew heavy and she drifted to sleep. She snapped awake only when the tyres crunched on gravel as they left the main road. They turned into a sweeping drive and the headlights swept over a large timber entry portico with an enormous peaked roof. Mr. Yi got out and moved around the car to open Hazel's door. Both children climbed out and stood, mouths agape, at the vast stone house that stretched out endlessly in every direction and seemed to disappear into a grove of soaring black-green pines. Mr. Yi retrieved their bags from the boot and led them to the doors. As she passed into the silent house, Hazel had the odd sensation of coming home.

"Please follow me," he said, leading them through the doors into a grand entry hall. A large staircase with dark, twisted banisters wrapped around two sides of the hall. The roof soared three stories high and was framed by thick timbers. Hazel stopped short and stared in fascination and disgust. Taxidermy animals were mounted everywhere on the walls: deer, gazelle, moose, rhino and one spotted animal with four twisted horns and small tusks that Hazel had never even imagined. She roused herself and looked back at Mr. Yi, who was observing her. Hazel felt self-conscious about the disgusted look on her face and smiled weakly.

Mr. Yi shook his head slightly and said, "Barbaric. But they have been here for as long as anyone can remember. It never hurts to consider how things have been and might be again." He placed their bags at the foot of the stairs and beckoned them through heavy double doors into a spectacular dining room.

The vast room was lit only by a roaring fire within a heavy stone hearth, leaving the far corners in shadow. High above, chandeliers made of antlers hung darkly and a small shadowy balcony ringed the room, one storey above. The dark, wood table, opposite the fireplace, was enormous. Although it could easily seat thirty or more, only two places were set for dinner.

"Will Mrs. Withersnips and her children not be joining us?" Hazel asked Mr. Yi as she took her seat.

"There are no other children here," replied Mr. Yi with his same unreadable look. "Mrs. Withersnips has a pressing concern this evening and will not be seeing you. She has left you a note. Please eat."

With that, Mr. Yi made a slight bow and hurried out of the room through a door Hazel had not previously noticed – likely because it was hidden behind a cabinet filled with old pistols.

"Well," Hazel said to Bec with a wry smile, "looks like we won't be cramped!" She ladled out bowls of thick soup for both of them, tore open a steaming roll, and began to read the note.

Miss. Benedict and Mr. Beckwith,

Welcome to Fairwarren. I regret not being able to greet you upon your arrival. So much to be done and I simply cannot spare the time. You must think of the house as your home whenever you are here. I am told there are lovely things to see here and I encourage you to look about, while you can. Mr. Yi will see that you have what you need. Kitty will be around to help and can always be relied upon to find a thing to eat when you need it. She says it is never a bad idea to carry snacks in case you find yourself away.

Yours,
W

At first Hazel read quickly and was left feeling a little confused. She then read it again and began to feel uneasy about a few points.

"What's it say?" mumbled Bec as he helped himself to more soup.

"Have a look," Hazel responded, passing the note with buttery fingers. Her confusion was momentarily lost in the delight of fresh butter, a rarity at home due to food rationing.

Bec took it, brows furrowing as he read, and then looked up at Hazel. "Why do we need to look around 'while we can'? Is Mrs. Withersnips going to send us away?" Bec asked.

"And why do we need snacks with us? Where are we meant to go?" Hazel added.

Bec shrugged but before they could debate any further, they felt a gentle tremor in the floor.

"What on earth?" Hazel asked grasping the sides of the table.

"Fascinating," Bec replied. "Tectonic activity in the Southern Great Lakes zone! Unusual. It's generally quite stable. I wonder if there is a library here; I'd love to find out more about the seismicity…"

Hazel gazed at Bec; head cocked to one side. The boy had a fact for every circumstance. Just then, Mr. Yi returned.

"It is time to withdraw to your rooms," he said as another slight tremor shook the floor. Mr. Yi's usually composed face looked tense.

"Are we quite safe?" asked Hazel as he approached.

"Safe," he replied in a tone that sounded to Hazel more like a question than an assurance. Mr. Yi ushered them from the room, asking them to stay close as he gathered their bags and turned up the stairs.

"What I meant to ask, is the house in danger? Earthquakes and all."

"Fairwarren is quite safe. Quite safe, for now," Mr. Yi responded calmly, but he was clearly rattled. Hazel and Bec were silent and Mr. Yi continued without referring again to the tremors. "Please try to take note of the way, I have many duties and will not be able to escort you regularly."

"Mr. Yi," asked Hazel, "are you quite well?" She gently touched his arm, which made him start.

"I am well. There is simply much to be done." Another small shake followed, and Mr. Yi quickened his footsteps.

Unfortunately, the conversation distracted her from the walk and she realised with regret that she had not been paying attention to where they were going. She needed to keep a closer watch if she was ever going to get back to the dining room.

The house was a maze. Doorways, stairs and corridors spun off in every direction. Many of the walls were panelled in dark wood, while others were covered in deep-hued paper in an ivy pattern. Every space was stuffed with furniture and curiosities that were continually pulling Hazel's gaze away from where she was walking. Her mum would sniff and call it 'cluttered', but Hazel was dazzled.

Where they went next, Hazel could not say. She counted four corridors and two further sets of stairs – one they went up and the other down in another direction. At the intersection of two staircases and a hall, Mr. Yi directed Bec to wait and he hurried off with Hazel close behind – without a moment to bid her friend goodnight.

Mr. Yi opened an ornately carved door off a narrow passage with windows on one side. Hazel was pleasantly surprised to find a sizeable room, warmly lit by a fire in the hearth. The chill of autumn was in the air and Hazel sighed at the cosiness.

"You will find what you need here," said Mr. Yi, placing her case on a trunk at the foot of a large, inviting bed. "Anything you find in this room is for your use. Sleep well." And with that he left, pulling closed the heavy door.

Hazel took in the welcoming comfort of the room. Two tall windows stood across from the door, each with a small seat set into the opening. The four-poster bed, across from the hearth, was almost too high to climb into. On one side of the bed stood a dark cupboard with a mirror set into it and on the other, a narrow door was cracked open to reveal her very own bathroom. Her own home didn't even have an indoor toilet, let alone one of her own.

Despite the pleasantness of the room, Hazel was suddenly overwhelmed by loneliness. She determined to locate Bec and bid him goodnight – and perhaps get some reassurances about the disturbing tremors. There had been no prohibition about leaving her room, but she nevertheless did so quietly. She found her way back to the spot where Mr. Yi had left Bec and began to look around, trying to guess in which direction they might have gone. A narrow flight of stairs drew her attention and she decided to try it.

At the top, she found a wide octagonal landing with doors on each side. She realised she might well have been wrong about which direction Bec and Mr. Yi had taken and was about to lose her nerve when the third door opened and a pyjama-clad Bec stuck his head out.

"Oh, hi Haze!" he said cheerfully, as if he had been expecting to find her by his room.

Hazel stared back at him with a funny look on her face.

"What's wrong?" he asked nervously, wiping at his face with the back of his hand. "Is there something on me?"

"No, nothing. Only, you called me Haze," she replied in a dreamy voice.

"Oh sorry," Bec replied, wondering how he had offended her.

"I've just never had a nickname before," she replied with a flush.

"It's all right then?"

"Yes, it's all right. Really all right. Where were you going?"

"Rather wanted to say goodnight, you know."

"Me too!" grinned Hazel.

"Well come in, you really should see my room."

Bec seemed suddenly embarrassed at the suggestion the moment he said it and continued hurriedly, "It has an incredible book collection, I mean. I've been reading about some extraordinary concepts in spatial physics; another one has a hypothetical look into history, had the Roman Empire not fallen. Actually a bit confusing, but incredible. I mean, I've never seen books covering any of these topics before – not one!"

"The whole place is a bit confusing!" Hazel agreed as she followed him into his room.

But as soon as she was inside, Hazel realised how tired she was and, comforted at knowing where her friend was in this vast and unfamiliar house, she said, "Look, I better get to bed. We won't figure it all out tonight."

"S'pose," Bec muttered as he flipped a few more pages of a book. "Glad you came to me, probably I was never going to find you. This place really is a warren!"

"It's not so bad," Hazel responded. "I'm starting to get a feel for it."

Hazel caught sight of a small bell on Bec's bedside table and picked it up. It was barely bigger than a thimble but when Hazel gave it a shake it let out a cheerful chime.

"Take it with you for breakfast; if you get confused give it a ring and I'll come and find you," Hazel offered. "Directions are my one superpower," she grinned.

"Good to know. Mine is useless facts!" he replied sheepishly and gestured toward the open suitcase of books on his bed.

Before she reached the door, Bec called out, "There is certainly something peculiar here, but I'll tell you what, it seems far better than vegetonians in Orillia and I'm really, really glad we ended up together."

"Me too, Bec. Me too. 'Night," Hazel said, and slipped back to her room.

Settling onto the edge of her large bed she gazed about the room with its soft chairs, large wardrobe and book-filled shelves. It was a delight after the nights in the cramped boat and the train. The mystery of her new home and her hosts still played over in her mind but knowing that Bec was close by under this roof, she burrowed under her covers and slept.

FOUR

azel awoke, vaguely aware of a noise rousing her. She struggled to emerge from the downy softness of her bed, reached for the beside light and looked at the clock. It was five. While it would soon be light, it was too early for the household to be up. As she sat up, shaking the sleep out of her head, Hazel again heard the sound that woke her; it was the gentle tinkling of Bec's bell!

Hazel rushed to the door and threw it open, trying to discern the direction of the ringing. Her eyes began to grow accustomed to the dark and the vaguest tinge of grey penetrated the darkness, helping her find her way. Hazel dashed to the right, away from the stairs, and heard the tinkling growing louder. She was slightly alarmed, given the hour, but also a little annoyed. How could Bec get himself lost three hours before breakfast?

Hazel reached the end of her hall, turned in the

direction of the bell and dashed up a few steps. She crossed a large gallery and turned down another hall until she came to a large set of double doors blocking the passage. The top halves of the doors were glass and through this Hazel beheld an impossible scene. In front of her stretched a corridor that wound away for such a length that the end could not be made out. Closely spaced doors lined both sides – each utterly different from the next. And though she knew it could not be so, it seemed this corridor must stretch for miles.

Just as she backed away from the double doors, a body crashed into hers and knocked her to the ground. "Oof," she grunted, rolling over. It was Bec, dressed in pyjamas and a rumpled dressing gown.

"What in heavens?" she asked, tidying her nightgown.

"Awfully sorry," Bec apologised, sitting up from where he had fallen after her. "I heard your bell ringing and I followed the sound and it kept moving faster and faster. I was at a total sprint when I turned that last corner. Why were you running away?"

"I wasn't!" Hazel retorted, getting to her feet. "I was just standing here."

"Oh," was all Bec could think to say. "But wait, what are you doing walking about at this hour anyway?" he enquired a little sharply.

"Looking for you! Your bell woke me up and I've been hunting for you. I don't even have a bell."

"But I haven't mine either. Forgot it! How did we each end up chasing one another, do you figure?" Bec asked, looking along the bizarre corridor.

"No clue. This place gets more peculiar by the minute. I think we should get back to bed though. I can't imagine we're meant to be wandering before light."

"Yeah, okay," Bec hesitated, then continued. "But, do you think you can help me find my room? I know I should be able to retrace my steps, but I used to end up in the kitchen when I was trying to find the billiard room in my own house," he laughed. "Truly and utterly hopeless with directions."

"I don't think you are the best companion for life at Fairwarren then," Hazel said with a wry smile, recounting the mess of hallways she encountered during the evening.

"Indeed," said a hushed but clear voice from a dark doorway.

"Who's that?" shrieked Bec. Hazel and Bec both stepped back in surprise and exchanged worried glances, neither certain if they had broken a rule wandering about in the night.

A tall woman moved into the light. She wore a grey woollen skirt and a faded mauve cardigan. Thick-framed glasses hung around her neck on a golden chain. It was difficult to say how old she was. Her thin frame and hazy grey-brown hair were in contrast to her smooth face and sparkling green eyes. "I think you will find that we've given you just exactly the companion you need," she continued, moving to sit in a throne-like chair against the wall.

"I beg your pardon," Hazel said timidly. "We're ever so sorry. Are you, perhaps, Mrs. Withersnips?"

"The one. Well then," she said, after nibbling on a square of chocolate she procured from her pocket, "let's have a look at the both of you. Yes, I like the look of you well enough.

More than that other lot from England, was that twelve years ago? I mean, they did their best, didn't they? But the one was so very doughy and the other, well there is something to be said for using a handkerchief, is there not?"

Finding the children speechless, she continued, "So, you've found it. What do you think?"

Hazel wrung her hands together nervously as she answered. "I beg your pardon, but what exactly have we found?"

"Why the Corridor, of course. Yi, are we really going to have to start at the beginning?" Mrs. Withersnips sighed.

Hazel and Bec started as they saw Mr. Yi, as tidy and formal as ever, approaching from yet another hallway.

"As always, Madame, we must," he replied with a bow and what Hazel thought was a small roll of his eyes.

"Follow me, then," said Mrs. Withersnips turning away from the strange corridor. She walked back toward the main staircase and opened a large set of doors at the landing. When they entered, Hazel gasped. They were in an expansive library, with thousands of books lining the walls on two levels. Bec let out a low whistle and moved to a nearby shelf, immediately lost in the titles. Hazel heard Bec muttering to himself, "Antipodean Invertebrates, ooh and a biography of Attila the Hun and…"

"Umm, do you think it might be possible for you to explain?" Hazel asked in a small, nervous voice, ignoring Bec's recitation of titles.

Bec recalled himself and moved to Hazel's side. "Yes, exactly what the dickens is going on?" he added, drawing himself up and trying to sound imposing.

"Well then, tempers can be expected to flair around the Corridor but do try to keep your language in check, dear," Mrs. Withersnips said, smiling thinly at Bec. She gestured to a set of four leather armchairs set in a niche near the library's windows. Outside, the sky was beginning to turn purple. The children sat next to each other, and Mrs. Withersnips sat across a small table from them. Mr. Yi paced in front of the stacks.

"Yi, why don't you begin. I do hate to begin," said Mrs. Withersnips, closing her eyes and settling back into the leather.

"Many hundreds of years ago..." began Mr. Yi, but Mrs. Withersnips cleared her throat.

"Do you need to begin such a long time ago? We'll miss breakfast," she said, not opening her eyes.

Mr. Yi sighed and walked over to a cabinet near the windows. He returned and placed a newspaper on the table between them. The headline read: *Squadron of Planes Vanishes Over Belgium. RAF Provides no Explanation.* The children took a moment to read and then exchanged worried, but not surprised, expressions.

"You have read this before?" Mr. Yi asked, slightly suspiciously.

Bec and Hazel looked at one another, trying to decide what to say. Clearly, this was not a normal household, but if they revealed what they had seen, would they be sent away as troublemakers, or liars?

"Yes, on the train. Some boys had the paper," Hazel replied carefully.

"Then perhaps you would be interested in these?" Mr. Yi placed a large selection of newspapers on the table, one at a time. Some headlines were in English and others were in foreign languages, but the ones they could read reported the same sort of events. People or vehicles – in some cases buildings – vanishing into nothing.

"What is causing it?" Bec asked.

"The papers say electrical storms," Mr. Yi answered, looking closely at the children's faces. "They are wrong."

They looked at him expectantly.

"These rifts are happening when another world collides with our own," he said matter-of-factly.

"Beg your pardon but did you say, 'another world'—?" began Hazel as she looked between the adults nervously.

"Yi, get to it so we can minimise interruptions and tedious questions," Mrs. Withersnips interjected again.

"Many years ago – long before any of us – it was discovered that other worlds, which we call Wards, were splintering from our own. They pull apart from us but remain tethered to our world. So, each time a Ward is created, our own grows more unstable. These Wards then evolve on their own from the moment they split; their own unique histories unfolding. This monstrous war in Europe may be due, in part, to a massive splintering event. If the Wards grow too unstable, they may begin to shift – bumping, if you will, up against our own world. Those are the rifts you have read about."

"But—" Hazel began again.

"Please Miss Benedict, listen. Unable to stop the splinters, or the rifts, our predecessors developed ways to try to minimise them and to stabilise the worlds when the rifts occurred. We Wardens," he gestured to Mrs. Withersnips and himself, "direct the efforts to create stability. Here at

Fairwarren, through the Corridor you just saw, the splintered Wards can be reached. By installing or fixing devices, called Obcasix, in the Wards, we can help stabilise the worlds, protecting us and them from danger."

Mr. Yi stopped talking and a thick silence filled the room. Hazel's heart thudded so loudly in her chest she was sure the others could hear it. She thought back to the scene from the boat, to the tremors in the house, to the newspapers, and felt herself believing. She and Bec had been so afraid of being mocked or scolded for revealing what they saw and now here were adults waiting for her to believe even more fanciful tales.

"We saw one," she blurted out. "We saw a rift on the ship and through the crack there was a city. Huge and unrecognisable, like from a dream."

Mrs. Withersnips gave Mr. Yi a probing look.

"Why don't the reports talk about that?" Hazel asked.

"No one can see the other Wards," Mr. Yi explained. "They can see the effects on our world, but not the other Wards themselves."

"But we saw it, we saw it plain as day. It was black as pitch on the ocean, but daylight there. Sun reflected off of really tall towers. It was clear," Hazel protested, "you can't say it can't be seen."

"You misunderstand me," Mr. Yi corrected. "Other people can't see through. You can see the other side. You and Mr. Beckwith – you are Rangers."

"You mean like a Girl Guide?" Bec snapped. "I am not a Girl Guide!" He looked at Mr. Yi and then leapt up and cut a furious path back and forth across the carpet. But something in his tone was more pleading than angry.

"We Wardens," Mr. Yi continued, "can oversee the Obcasix and the Wards in some ways but we cannot enter the Wards to fix them. Only Rangers can do that. They are unique individuals with the ability to cross between Wards. Rangers are always under the age of eighteen; young minds can weather the shift in perspective, adults cannot."

Bec fell back into a chair and hung his head low over his knees. Then, he covered his ears with his hands and shook his head, as if trying to block a painful noise. Mrs. Withersnips crossed over to him and gently, though clumsily, patted his head but said nothing.

Hazel looked at Bec across the table, his skin shimmering slightly in the lamplight. She thought about how only she and Bec had seen the rift and something slid into place. There was a reason she had always felt different! It just wasn't a reason she could have ever dreamed.

At that moment, the library doors burst open and an extremely short, round woman came bustling into the room. She wore an old-fashioned floor-length dress that looked rather like a nightie and her thick black hair hung in a heavy plait well past her ample behind.

"Tea!" she said in a cheerful voice, as she pushed a trolley that emitted the fragrant smell of scones.

"Hello chums," she said, addressing the children. "I'm named Kitty, and I run this here house, no matter what Yi says." She jerked her chin in the direction of Mr. Yi whose calm features did not change at all.

"We have rather a lot to get through, Kitty dear," Mrs. Withersnips said with a sigh. "Yi is rather insistent."

"Indeed you do," Kitty replied, "but it will wait for tea."

Much to Bec and Hazel's surprise, the two Wardens made no further protest, and all was silent while the meal was served.

FIVE

Only minutes passed as Kitty handed around cups of steaming tea. Hazel breathed heavily as she tried to get her mind around what Mr. Yi had just said. They were being told that their world periodically splintered, forming new worlds, and that young people, like her and Bec, had to move through them fixing devices that were needed to maintain stability. They were being told that the bizarre vision they saw on the ship was a real place. Hazel looked at her cup of tea and then back up at Kitty.

"You'll find that the wonders never cease around these parts so you may as well get used to it and keep something nourishing in you all the while."

"Does this have something to do with our shimmering?" Hazel asked, thinking about the conversation she'd had on deck with Bec. She pointed to the skin on her arm.

"Indeed," continued Mr. Yi, "it is the mark of a Ranger

– one that only other Rangers can see. Though we have ways of detecting it." He pulled the monocle from his pocket. "You were both born with a unique link to the energy of the Wards. It is rare. That connection leaves this mark. We at Fairwarren are charged with tracking people who have the ability and putting in place the mechanisms for them to come and join us here. It is unusual to have two English children marked at the same time but happily it wasn't as difficult as it sometimes is to direct you both here thanks to the evacuee programme," Mr. Yi explained.

"Though clearly with some bumps along the way," added Mrs. Withersnips rolling her eyes at Mr. Yi. "The boy could have been stuck in Orillia for weeks! And the girl, good lord, her parents wanted to send her to Inverness. Inverness, can you imagine? What the devil use would she be to anyone in Scotland?"

"One moment!" Hazel cried, standing. "Are you telling us that you brought us here on purpose, that you tricked our parents?"

"We facilitate you getting to where you need to be. The children come to us when they are needed; we provide whatever assistance we can. We had some work to do to figure out how to get you here. The boy, not as much – his parents sent him this way in a flash," Mrs. Withersnips continued, apparently unaware of the sting of her words.

Bec's shoulders slumped but he didn't look very surprised. "So, you say we are marked? For what exactly?" Bec asked.

"For training as Rangers and maintaining the stability of the Wards, of course," snapped Mrs. Withersnips from her chair. "Pay attention."

"What if the children don't want to? What if they just want to stay at home, in their own world or whatever? Do you simply steal them?" Hazel grew angrier as she spoke. She might feel there was something right about this place, but she didn't like feeling tricked. What had the Wardens done to make her parents send her away?

"My dear girl," replied Mrs. Withersnips, getting to her feet and leaning in toward Hazel, "not a single child has ever been made to stay here against their will. Nor has one ever asked to leave. I don't think you want to either. Being a Ranger is who you are and have been since birth. You did not know how you were different, or how you were needed, but you felt a hole inside that called for purpose. Now you can fill that hole."

Hazel felt slightly nauseous. She was somehow certain that this was all true and she sensed that very, very soon they would be in grave danger. One look at Bec made her certain he felt the same. Nonetheless, she was going to need more information.

"So our world," she gestured all around, "is sort of the main world and lots of others broke away from it? And, you all run some sort of control booth? Bec and I need to be sent out into those other worlds to do some engineering and then what? What happens if we don't?"

"Good lord, you do ask a lot of questions!" Mrs. Withersnips complained. She tucked into a third scone, gesturing to Mr. Yi to continue.

"You have the general idea, Miss. Benedict – if somewhat crudely explained. If the rifts, like the one you saw, continue, the very fabric of our world could unravel. Global destruction would follow. We have no idea what that would look like, but it is not an option. This war would seem like a holiday in comparison."

"And the other Wards?" Hazel asked, her voice cracking a little with tension.

"While they exist, as much as you and me, the splintered worlds are more fragile. A significant impact could obliterate them."

"Whole worlds? With all their people?" Hazel asked, tears coming to her eyes.

"I am afraid so," replied Mr. Yi solemnly.

"But why, why is all this happening now?" asked Hazel.

"Well, dear, we really do need to tell you about Eris," said Kitty brightly as she poured more tea.

Mr. Yi sighed and began again, "As we explained, we Wardens are charged with keeping the Wards stable at all costs. But there are others who want the Wards to split. In a way, the other Wards, the splinters, take something of our world with them when they split. Only by tethering ourselves to them, with the help of the Obcasix, can we remain stable. Others believe the worlds being broken apart and permanently severed is the natural order. The entity most set on this outcome goes by the name Eris. She believes the splintered worlds suck life from our own, steadily bleeding us. She would split the Wards apart – forever. It is possible that the rifts are being caused by Eris or one of her minions."

Bec, who had been uncharacteristically quiet, gulped and said, "Minions?"

"Rangers can navigate through the energy in and between the Wards, but they cannot manipulate it. Eris, however, has found a way to control that energy. She uses it to create creatures who can do her bidding where she cannot. We believe, though we are not sure, that she herself may have been mutated somehow by the energy. She has been growing more powerful, learning ways to impact the Wards even we never dreamt of. What's more, she has recruited some young people, like yourselves, to work on her behalf."

"But could she be right? I mean, should the worlds really be connected if it causes so much trouble?" Hazel asked. The Wardens turned to her, their faces masks. Hazel felt self-conscious but she carried on, "I don't understand any of this, but if it takes devices and children and all of this to maintain," she gestured to Fairwarren around her, "is there something wrong with the system?"

Mrs. Withersnips replied, her voice tight, "Philosophical debate for another time. Without the other Wards, the other parts of us, we would erode and fracture to nothing. To nothing! Do you see? Eris is an enigma; we don't understand her yet but we know that she wants destruction and chaos. The end of all."

Hazel wasn't absolutely sure she did see, but her body began to shiver all over, and she no longer wanted to think about the end.

In that moment, the library bucked and rolled, books danced on their shelves, some falling to the floor.

"Curses, Yi, it's getting bad," snapped Mrs. Withersnips as she clutched the back of a chair. "Faster than we thought!" she added.

Mr. Yi nodded tersely and continued, "Our other two Rangers have not returned from their last assignment. Their absence, and that of the Obcasix they carry, may also be causing some of this disturbance," Mr. Yi explained quickly, gesturing to the tousled library. "If their work is not completed or they are lost, the results for the Wards could be dire."

"Fairwarren is special," Mrs. Withersnips said, panting as if out of breath. "Here, the barrier between the Wards is thin, making it one of a very few places where the connection to the Wards is managed. A constant in the ever-shifting worlds. However, when things become unduly unstable in the Wards, as they are now, the house can be affected. It is not normal and suggests a serious problem."

Bec snorted and repeated, "Normal, yeah right!"

Standing by a bookshelf, Hazel reached out a hand to steady herself. She inhaled deeply to calm herself and it began to dawn on her that she was both scared and excited but that she believed every word.

Hazel looked over at Bec whose face was turning disturbingly red. She wanted to go to him, comfort him and tell him it was all right, but she had no clue why she thought it was. She just knew that from the moment she entered Fairwarren she had felt strangely right.

A hush fell over the library as its occupants seemed to contemplate what had just been said. Finally, Hazel spoke, "May I just be clear? What you are saying is that Bec and I need to cross into another world to find two missing people we've never met and if we don't, our world, and others, may risk destruction?"

"It does sound a bit dire when you state it like that," said Mrs. Withersnips. "But yes, that is the general idea."

"And we have to go without any help?" Hazel asked.

"I'll pack sandwiches, dear," Kitty replied.

"Yes," Mr. Yi stepped in. "Wardens can't go in. You must go alone."

"But if we manage it, will the war end and our families be safe?" Hazel asked.

"Dear girl," said Kitty soothingly, "we must keep the worlds from fracturing into nothing. But we cannot control what the people within them do. People are still people, with their fears and their hatred, but also with their love and compassion. If you succeed, at least our world will have the chance to mend itself."

"But the training!" Mrs. Withersnips growled as another quake shook the room.

"Things are growing worse faster than we thought; they need to go now, unprepared though they are," Mr. Yi replied. To the children, he asked in a strained tone they had not yet heard, "Are you willing? Will you go?"

Bec and Hazel looked at each other as waves of confusion crashed over them. There was almost too much information to absorb for rational thought but after a moment, their eyes locked on one another and they both said, "Yes."

Then, the house bucked yet again and Bec fell to the floor.

"There is so much more to explain," Mrs. Withersnips said, standing, "but time is of the essence – prepare yourselves. Clothes and supplies are in your rooms."

"Now, now, they haven't had their breakfast," Kitty tutted.

"Kitty, we have something of a situation, dear," said Mrs. Withersnips, tidying her plain clothes and checking her hair. "We must investigate these recent tremors before they can go to the Corridor and they need to get ready."

"That they do," nodded the round woman, "so be off, ya skinny old bat, see what Eris has wrought, but the kiddos stay and eat."

"Bah," was the only response from Mrs. Withersnips, who seemed remarkably unconcerned by this behaviour. She and Mr. Yi headed to the door with a quick backward glance. "At the Corridor, half an hour." With that, they hurried out of the library.

"Right then, eat yer fill," said Kitty, wheeling the cart over to the table. She unveiled a wonderful spread of eggs, fried potatoes and bacon from which they hurriedly filled their plates. Despite their raw nerves, the food was irresistible.

"Only moments ago, we were told the most incredible things that no sane person should believe," Bec commented, "and here we are eating as if it were the most ordinary of breakfasts!"

"I'll beg your pardon, young man, I'll not countenance anyone calling my breakfast ordinary," Kitty declared, but a warm smile was breaking across her round face.

Kitty lifted the cloth over the cart to reveal another shelf. From this she pulled out two paper bags and handed one to each of the children. "For your packs. Can't ever know for certain where you'll be, and for how long, so it's imperative to have some supplies."

Kitty began to tidy up while the children stood, bags in hand and mouths agape.

"But Kitty," said Hazel, "we have no idea where to start or how to recognise the Rangers or Eris."

"And how on earth do we know what to pack?" added Bec.

"Too many questions, you two. Ever heard of a story where the answers came at the beginning?" replied Kitty unhelpfully. Then, seeing the terrified looks on the children's faces, she sat down on the table between them.

"Look here. We are indeed in a mighty worrying moment and the Wardens would never normally send you into danger unprepared. But I know two things for certain. The first is that if they're sending you in it is because they have no choice. The second is that Rangers are special. You came into the world that way, even if you didn't know it. Here you are, two days off the boat from England and you are getting ready to enter other worlds. If you were two ordinary children you'd be crying for your mummies and hiding in your rooms. Yes?"

The two exchanged looks but her words made some sense. They were each incredulous, but they were still planning to do what the Wardens asked. There must be something to that.

"Keep your eyes open and trust yourselves. You know more than you think. Now, off to your rooms. Bring your packs and hurry back to the Corridor lest you keep them waiting. Tetchy pair those two when something needs doing!" Kitty declared and swatted them with her dish towel.

Hazel and Bec left the library and made their way down the hallway.

"I feel sick," said Bec.

"Nerves or bacon?" asked Hazel.

Bec burped again and said, "Honestly, both. Haze, do you think we should run? I mean, pack our bags and hit the road? Our parents wouldn't send us here if they thought the adults were going to launch us into something dangerous."

"Bec," Hazel said carefully, "I know it all seems utterly mad, but it feels oddly right. With the war and with so many people dying, I've been thinking I wanted to – needed to – do something. It was like what Mrs. Withersnips said, I had an itch I couldn't scratch that never went away. Ever since we arrived, I don't feel it anymore. It's as if I am finally doing something."

She looked down at her shoes. It was a little embarrassing to tell Bec that. She didn't want it to sound as though she thought she was a hero. She looked back up.

"I won't blame you if you don't want to go, though," she said. "This could all be a weird joke, or it could be something really dangerous. Either way, it's a risk. I wouldn't know what to do without you, but…" she looked at the floor again, "I would understand if you don't want to go!"

"Hold on there," Bec cried, gently grabbing hold of her shoulders. "You aren't getting rid of me. It's an absolute brain-melter, I'll admit, but deep down it doesn't feel wrong. What kind of best friend would I be if I let you go alone? I dare say we are going to need each other before this is through. We're a team!"

"A team," Hazel repeated and turned away. As afraid as she was, hearing Bec say "best friend" had filled her with happiness and she felt calm.

The Rangers stood in front of the Corridor. Each carried a leather pack filled to bursting. Mrs. Withersnips stood in front of them, looking slightly unkempt. Her tight, grey bun was tousled, and her cardigan was buttoned wrong. Mr. Yi, on the other hand, looked as precise and tidy as ever. And, to their surprise, Kitty was with them.

Mr. Yi stepped forward. "As we have indicated, this is highly irregular. We usually have an opportunity to train our Rangers at length, and to explain the procedures. We have no such opportunity with you. The situation is too serious to wait; we likely have only days, if that.

"Find, if you can, Anika and Joe, the last Rangers to enter the Corridor. A Ranger is like medicine – a small dose can save a life but too much can cause fatal consequences. If one of the Rangers has become stuck or –" Mr. Yi looked uncomfortably at Mrs. Withersnips "– has decided to stay, they will begin to cause problems that may partially explain the shifts we have been feeling."

"Wait!" Hazel protested. "How will we know them? How can we recognise Eris if she's out there? How do we fight her? Where do we go? How do we get back?" Hazel's resolve was failing in the face of so many unanswered questions.

Mr. Yi stepped toward them again. "Pay close attention to where you arrive. Your only way back is through the same door," he said to Hazel, but his eyes darted to Bec. She understood that his tendency to get lost might well be a liability. She would have to stay close.

Mr. Yi reached into his pocket and pulled out two rings. Each was a simple flat band in a dull metal Hazel could not name; at the top, three circles formed a tiny bull's eye pattern. "Wear these and never take them off. Your own energy and these rings are the keys to your re-entry to Fairwarren. They should never leave your fingers."

Hazel and Bec slipped on their rings and exchanged uncertain looks.

"And, take this," said Mrs. Withersnips, pressing a small leather notebook into Hazel's hand. It was well worn and held together by a length of frayed string. "It's the Ranger journal. A place for Rangers to share their findings and thoughts. It could help." She ushered them into the Corridor.

"But," said Bec looking down the endless expanse, "which door do we take?"

"That is for the Rangers to decide. You will know," replied Mr. Yi. As he closed the double doors behind them. He added, "The Corridor will help guide you, it is intentional in its choices."

Hazel and Bec stared nervously at the closed doors before turning and advancing down the endless hall, their footsteps silent on the thick carpet. They looked from side to side at the closed doors. Each was different: One had misty glass at the top, another was a dark ebony and looked worm-eaten and ancient, another had a number on it like in a hotel.

"How on earth will we know?" Bec asked, going over to a door and putting his hand on it. "Should we just try one and have a peek?" He moved his hand to the knob. Hazel called out, "Stop!" But she could see that his hand was shaking too much to turn it. Much like herself, Bec seemed to be pretending more confidence than he felt.

"I think," she said, "I think we will know it when we see it."

They walked on for a long time in silence, passing by dozens of doors with no end to the Corridor in sight. Without warning, Hazel stopped so abruptly that Bec, who had been staring at the doors on the right, crashed into her.

"Sorry," he mumbled, embarrassed, as he pulled himself back.

"This is the one," Hazel said, standing in front of a very ordinary door painted white with a frosted window set in the top half.

"Doesn't look like much, does it?" said Bec, drawing a little closer. Then he added, "Oh, I see!" The door was glowing slightly – nothing dramatic, just the faint aura of light surrounded it – a bit like the glow they could see around one another.

Hazel turned from the door to Bec. "We don't know what to expect so I think we need to have some rules in place."

"Such as?" asked Bec, looking nervously at the door.

"OK. First, we stick together. No splitting up to make the search faster or such things. Second, if either of us is, you know... taken, the other should get back to the door as quickly as possible and try to get help. Third... I can't think of a third."

"Maybe we should stick with two! Quite a lot to process already!" Bec added.

"Right," said Hazel. She reached for the doorknob. Knowing hesitation might cause her to freeze, she turned the knob and pushed. There was a rush of warm air and they were immediately surrounded by a thick grey mist. As they stepped in Bec said, "Remember 'first', we stick together," and he took Hazel's hand and squeezed it tight.

SIX

As soon as Hazel and Bec moved forward, the door snapped shut behind them. The mist cleared, revealing an identical door just ahead, which they passed through. Looking around, they saw what appeared to be a hospital hallway. Hazel had only been to hospital once, three years before when her appendix ruptured and had to be removed. It was frightening and hurt a great deal, but the staff had been kind and she thought well of hospitals. This hallway looked very similar. It was painted light green and the door they had just left, like all the others, was white with a frosted glass window. A few gurneys were resting along the walls next to a row of locked medical cabinets that held gauze and other supplies. There was nothing unusual about any of it as far as Hazel could tell.

Before moving farther along, Hazel took some paper from her pack. A small plaque above the door from which they had come read '1255' and she wrote the number down. She had no idea whether things would be as confusing here as they were at Fairwarren, but she wasn't going to trust her memory. Just then, a door at the end of the hallway opened and a uniformed nurse stepped out. She turned and gave them a passing look then walked briskly away. *At least*, thought Hazel, *we don't appear to stand out in any particular way.*

Bec and Hazel set off in the same direction as the nurse in the hope she would lead them out of the hospital. They hadn't spoken a single word since coming through the door, and Hazel wondered if her voice even worked. The stillness of the hospital made her uneasy, but she remained silent.

As they turned from the hallway into a wide foyer, the children felt, rather than saw, movement behind them. Turning quickly, they caught a glimpse of a silvery shape passing into one of the patient rooms. They only saw it for a moment, but Hazel thought the shape lacked solidity; it was both fluid and airy, as if it were made of molten smoke. Whatever it was gave Hazel a confused feeling of both desire and repulsion and she wondered if it was the same form she had seen in the rift over the Atlantic.

"Did you see that?" Bec whispered in her ear and she nodded slightly. "Wasn't a person, was it?" he asked in a tone that clearly indicated he wanted to be assured that it was.

"N-no," stammered Hazel. "I do think, I really do think, we should get out of here." Bec nodded his agreement and they turned and began to walk quickly down the hall. Again, sensing movement behind, their walk became a run as they spun down a stairway next to a sign marked 'Exit'. In their hurry they crashed headlong into a pair of doctors.

"I beg your pardon!" said an older, grey-haired man with a German accent. "Have you no sense? Running like that in a hospital. This isn't the schoolyard!"

"All right then, Hedler," said a younger man soothingly. "An accident. Do be a bit careful, children." He had a soft voice, a kind face and an English accent. "What are you two doing at St. Thomas's?" he asked kindly, but with a hint of suspicion.

"Uncle," shrieked Bec a little too loudly. "Ah, visiting a sick uncle." *Heavens*, thought Hazel, *he isn't a very good liar.*

"Our mother asked us to come and bring him some books but now we're on our way home. Really need to be hurrying along, Dennis." Hazel took over the tale as she grabbed Bec's hand and pulled him toward the large, glass doors ahead in the lobby.

"Sorry," she said to the doctors over her shoulder as they hurried out into a cool, cloudy day.

They crossed the street in front of the hospital and entered a small park. From where they stood they could see the tower at the Houses of Parliament just to the north.

"London!" exclaimed Bec looking around. "Haze, this isn't Canada! We're in London. We're back in England. We could go see our families."

Bec paused then added, "Oh, of course not. But do you think we're in our own Ward but just back home?"

"I don't think so," Hazel said looking around. "Look at the city, the buildings, the cars. There aren't any signs of the army, no bomb damage, no blackout cloths. Everything is calm, it doesn't look like there is a war on here at all. And that doctor, do you think a London hospital would employ a German doctor while we are at war?"

They both collapsed onto a bench and looked at one another. England not at war? Hazel almost couldn't believe it. She had spent time in London with her parents visiting family and running errands. She had been there only months before when they dropped her sister off to work as a nurse. She had seen the city's residents and businesses board their windows, pile sandbags and live in terror of the whistle of incoming bombs. She had somehow been prepared for the places they went to be bizarre, but she hadn't imagined an England so similar to the one she had left weeks before and yet so different in this important way. After Mr. Yi's talk of the splintered Wards being fragile, she hadn't expected that they might be better!

"Look, we're going to need to find a newspaper and figure out what is happening here in this Ward," said Bec. "But first, what do you think was in the hospital corridor, and did it have anything to do with us?"

"Well," Hazel began nervously, "the Wardens did mention minions. I don't know what I pictured but it wasn't a lovely and terrifying smoke beast but maybe…" she trailed off thoughtfully.

"It was scary, wasn't it?" Bec asked but he seemed wistful as he said it. "Though, it was sort of beautiful. Silvery and smooth…" Bec's eyes had a longing look in them.

Hazel understood the feeling, but the way Bec seemed to be dreaming of it made her uneasy.

"Let's hurry and try to find the Rangers. Hopefully, the door brought us to more or less the right place. I mean, I hope they aren't in Peru or something!"

Hazel took the journal from Mrs. Withersnips out of her

pocket and began to flip through the pages. The book was a crowded and careless collection of notes and sketches in different ink and handwriting. Many words or illustrations were crossed out and annotated with new comments.

"Bec, look at this!" Hazel said, moving the book toward him. "It's a note about the Obcasix, with a sketch. The note is initialled J & A. Maybe something Joe and Anika wrote on a previous mission?"

The picture showed a thin disk, about the size of a jam jar lid, with concentric circles in different shades. Something shiny was set in the middle but it was hard to make out what was in the pencil sketch.

"At least we know what the thingy looks like," said Bec. "Too bad it didn't come with photos of the Rangers."

They looked back at the notebook. Stuck to the bottom of the page was a small reddish feather with a black streak down one side.

"That's from a Malagasy Flycatcher," Bec said excitedly, brushing the feather with his little finger. Blushing, he said, "Um, I think."

"How on earth?" Hazel responded, raising an eyebrow at her friend. After the initial excitement of his recognition, Bec hung his head and looked forlorn.

"Hey, what is it?" Hazel asked, concerned.

"Sometimes, when I was in trouble, my father would have me locked in a storage closet. After the third time, I thought to sneak in a torch so that the next time I wouldn't be in the dark. The room was pretty boring. Mostly old tins and drapes and such things. But once I had my torch, I found a set of birding guides. The pictures were beautiful, and I took to memorising them." Bec looked at the ground again. "I was in there a lot but only got to the Ps. Pied Monarch, I think."

"Oh, Bec!" Hazel said sympathetically, but seeing his discomfort, she nudged him and with a smile said, "Bloody good thing this wasn't from a Tawny Treesnipe then, eh?"

Bec smiled, "No such thing."

"What could it mean, do you think?" she asked. "Do you think it means we should go to Madagascar? That's what 'Malagasy' means, right? Can we even do that?"

"I'm not sure, but Mr. Yi did tell us that the Corridor doesn't act in an arbitrary way. If they were in Madagascar, why send us to London?"

Hazel stood up and began to pace in front of the bench. Suddenly she stopped. "A zoo!" she exclaimed, looking at Bec.

"God bless you," Bec said pleasantly.

"Not a sneeze, Bec, the London Zoo! Wouldn't that be the place you would find a Malagasy Flycatcher that isn't Madagascar?" Hazel suggested, but immediately began to doubt herself. "I mean it's probably a silly idea, the feather likely doesn't mean anything."

"No Haze, it's brilliant! And more importantly, it's all we've got. At least it might suggest a place they liked to go. Now, where is the zoo exactly?" Bec asked getting to his feet. His family spent almost half the year in London in a house in Belgravia, but the zoo was not the sort of place his parents ever took him.

"Regent's Park. I mean, assuming there is a London Zoo in this Ward and that it is in the same place." Hazel looked around energetically, her earlier disappointment and the unnerving shape in the hospital momentarily forgotten.

SEVEN

Moving away from the hospital, Hazel and Bec walked through the small park and out to the street. The River Thames opened up before them, glinting under the sunlight that pressed between the gathering grey clouds. London was much as they each remembered from their own Ward, but this version was utterly peaceful. There was nothing to suggest war or rationing or suffering. In fact, the city looked cleaner and greener than either recalled. Hazel turned back toward the hospital to check the landmarks and to be sure she knew how to get back – she caught a glimpse of silver moving between two trees.

"Bec, the thing! We need to hurry," she pleaded between her teeth.

They picked up the pace and hurried along the street for a street when Bec cried, "Bus!" Seeing a red double-decker pulling up alongside the curb, they jumped aboard the rear step just before it pulled away.

"It can't ride a bus can it?" he asked.

"No idea, but let's hope it doesn't move as fast as a vehicle," Hazel said as she climbed the stairs to the top and sank into a seat by the front window. There was no sign of the bizarre form on the pavement below them. The bus progressed down the street and they both sighed, sinking lower into the bench. Not long after, a woman sat in the seat next to them and the conductor walked up behind her.

"Tickets," he said tersely, and the lady passed him one absently. Bec and Hazel looked at each other nervously. They had both tucked some money into their packs before they left Fairwarren, but neither knew whether the money was the same here. If they pulled out a shilling from a different Ward it would surely get them in trouble. But the conductor didn't ask for their tickets, he just frowned and asked, "Travelling alone?"

"No. Well, not really, sir," replied Hazel quickly. "Our mum got off a few stops back for some shopping and sent us on home."

"Your mother is not meant to do that," said the conductor, still looking stern but clearly not seeing what he could do about the matter. The lady in the next seat was watching quietly and then turned and placed a gloved hand on the conductor's sleeve.

"We're neighbours. I can keep an eye on them. Happens often," she said with a sympathetic smile toward the teens.

The conductor gave a curt nod and walked back down the stairs as the bus started away from the station.

"Thank you," said Hazel. "We didn't think it would be a problem."

"No trouble dear. I needed some independence myself when I was your age." Then she caught sight of their backpacks. "Not running away though, are you? I won't sleep tonight if I thought I helped some young people into trouble."

"Oh, my, no," Hazel assured her. "We're just off to spend a few nights with father. They aren't together and she doesn't have time to take us back and forth. He said he'd meet us at the zoo." Bec was staring at his friend, completely amazed at the ease and confidence with which stories poured from her.

"I see," the woman said, nodding. "A lot of that these days, I'm afraid." It was only then that Bec noticed that this woman, like the doctor at the hospital, had a German accent.

They sat quietly watching the peaceful London streets roll by until about a half-hour later the woman reached a hand across the aisle and tapped Bec's arm. "Baker Street coming up next, my friends. From there it is a short walk to Regent's Park. The zoo is at the north end, you know. Will you be fine to find your papa and do you have an umbrella?" A steady rain had begun to coat the windows.

"Oh yes, certainly," replied Hazel with a smile. "We meet him there all the time; he lives nearby, in Primrose Hill."

"Auf Wiedersehen then," smiled the woman and Hazel and Bec said thank you as they went down the bus stairs, noting the German farewell. They hurriedly jumped off before they had to encounter the conductor who was at the back of the bus with a scowl on his face.

After a time, Bec began nervously, "Um, Hazel."

"Uh huh," she replied, still distracted by thoughts of home.

"How do you make up stories so well?" he asked.

Hazel turned to him and smiled sadly. She remembered all the times at home when, left to herself, she had created imaginary lives where things were easy and she never felt left out, odd, or alone. She also remembered all the fibs she told to excuse herself from family activities and to explain where she had been. To Bec, she simply replied, "Just good at make-believe, I guess."

When they reached the gate, the ticket seller pulled out his pocket watch and frowned. "Zoo closes in an hour; sure you want to pay for a ticket? Come back tomorrow maybe?"

Hazel pulled a sad face and said, "Oh dear, it did take us a rather long time to get here and we were so counting on a visit. We leave tomorrow, you see. Yes, we would like two tickets if you please, and we'll just do a quick turnaround. An elephant and such."

"Oh, go on then," said the man. "No ticket needed, seems such a waste so near to closing and in this rain."

"Thank you. Thank you ever so much!" exclaimed Hazel as they hurried inside. "Which way to the aviary? I do rather want to see a peacock."

"Straight ahead then right after the cat house. Enjoy. Make your way to the gates in time," the ticket collector added.

They hurried along as instructed but just as they passed the cat house the now familiar silver form caught their eye near the gate.

"No!" breathed Hazel. Despite its beauty, Hazel's fear of this unknown shadow was growing with each sighting.

"In here." Bec pulled Hazel into a house marked 'Reptiles'. They ran through the dark exhibit, weaving past cases of boas and tortoises, looking for a back way out. Though they could see little in the dim light, Hazel felt a strange prickling on her skin, as if an electric current was bouncing off her rain-moistened face. The feeling grew increasingly intense.

"Here!" shouted Bec. He pulled open a door marked 'Air Raid Shelter' and ran inside then slammed the door behind them.

"What are we doing in here?" whispered Hazel tensely. "Now we're trapped! It had to have seen us come in." Though there was no obvious sign that the thing had eyes, it was certainly able to track the Rangers.

"I saw it in the notebook before we left the park. There are safe spaces called Havens created where two Wards temporarily stick. The collision leaves a mark that doesn't seem to fit. A safe bubble frozen in time. I noticed the sign marked 'Air Raid Shelter' when we came in. There hasn't been a war here, remember. No fear of attack, so what is an air raid shelter doing in a zoo?"

"I really am happy you read as fast as you do!" Hazel said, relief in her voice.

They stood panting in the black room until Bec pulled a lighter from his pack.

"Wardens thought of everything," he said with a shrug when he saw Hazel's surprised expression in the flickering light.

They were expecting some sort of a bunker with block walls and maybe some emergency supplies. What they found was a small, cosy study. Two soft armchairs sat in the middle of a worn carpet. Bookshelves lined the walls and a small desk with a candle rested in the corner. Hazel took Bec's lighter and lit the candle. She looked over her shoulder at the door but all seemed safe for the moment – the thing was clearly unable to get in. It seemed the Havens could be accessed, or maybe even seen, only by Rangers.

Bec sank into a chair and exhaled, "Phew, that was a close one. I'd like to see that notebook again." Bec flipped through the journal, pausing from time to time to read in the dim light. "Haze, I think those things are called Weevers. I'm trying to get through some questionable handwriting to figure out if there is any way to get away from them."

Hazel continued to look around the room. There wasn't much to find. She went back to the desk but as she was replacing the candle, she noticed a book on a shelf, not far from the desk, that had a page marked with the same feather they had found in the Ranger journal.

"Oh!" exclaimed Hazel, making Bec look up.

"What's up?" he asked with a worried expression.

"Another Malagasy feather, right?" she said, holding it up for Bec to see. Then, she withdrew a sheet of paper from the page the feather had marked. She read the note written upon it.

A,
Paddington!
J.

Hazel nodded and looked back down at the note. "It could mean nothing, but maybe Joe is at Paddington and maybe they aren't even together. God, this is hopeless."

"Let's not panic. There have been lots of successful Rangers before us. There must be ways of getting around, of finding things, ways we just don't know yet. Let's focus on one thing at a time."

"Bec, look, there's a date on the note, it's only three days ago! We need to get out of here and get to Paddington Station. Maybe Joe will show up there again waiting for Anika. I wish we knew if that Weever is out there."

"Hold on, listen to this entry," Bec said, pointing to a page with a drawing of a Weever that made Hazel's skin crawl.

"The Weevers can't distinguish the Havens from regular places nor can they sense a Ranger when inside." Bec read from the journal entry, then turned to Hazel. "If this is true, it's not likely to just hang around a random door. It would be long gone by now. Haze, this journal is full of really helpful stuff. Maybe we should take a little time to read. The Wardens could have saved us a lot of trouble if they'd just given us time to study!"

Hazel kicked the small table next to the chair and sent it tumbling to the ground.

"This is just too hard!" she cried.

There were menacing creatures outside and she and Bec were looking for one boy and a girl among millions with no real idea how to proceed. And, despite all the fear and running, what had they really achieved so far except to cross a bit of London on a bus? It felt hopeless and the grownups who actually knew something weren't helping at all. She struggled with a deep urge to return to the Wardens and demand answers.

Bec continued to try to be encouraging, "Hazel, don't worry, I'm sure we aren't meant to have it all figured out yet. Let's just put one foot ahead of the next. We'll take some time and read through this journal. Then, if we need to, we could go back to Fairwarren and at least see if Mrs. Withersnips has a photograph of the Rangers. We know the way now and we could be really quick."

He leaned over to pick up the table Hazel had kicked, but when he did so a sudden lurching sensation came over the Rangers, like a rolling wave on the ocean; his hand passed clean through the table as if it were mist. They looked at each other in shock. The tremors at Fairwarren had prepared them a little for the disconcerting feeling but not for items around them to lose substance!

"I don't think we can stay!" Hazel shouted as another roll passed through the room and Bec fell to the floor as the chair he was leaning on flitted out of form.

"Ooof," he cried as he hit the floor with a thud.

The whole room seemed to shudder and waft in and out of sight around them, like a mirage.

"Let's get out!" Hazel shouted and grabbed her pack and the journal. She lunged for the door, Bec right behind her. They threw themselves out into the reptile house and pulled the door shut behind them. When they stopped to compose themselves and look around, the door they had just left was gone.

"What on earth just happened?" Bec asked, rubbing his leg where he had hit the floor.

"Haven't a clue!" Hazel replied. "But I really do think we should get going. No telling how far that Weever might have gone and it must be getting on toward closing. I'm not sure I want to spend the night in the reptile house."

"Nor I," said Bec stepping away from a glass case where a menacing-looking striped snake was pressed to the glass right behind him.

EIGHT

They slipped quietly out of the building into the gathering night. There were no signs of people, even though the rain had ceased for the time being. Hazel looked at her watch and saw that it was after seven. Closing time had passed and they were almost certainly locked in. They walked slowly through the zoo in the direction of the gates half-expecting to be tossed out by a guard, but they saw no one. They tried the door to the House of Mammals, but it was locked. As they walked along the perimeter fence, looking for another exit or a tree that would help them scale the fence, they heard a scraping sound behind them. They knew enough now to understand that Weevers made no sound, but the creatures were not their only worry.

"No reason to jump, duckies," said a lilting Irish accent. They spun around to find an elderly man pushing a creaking wagon. He looked as if he could be over one hundred years old but with a head of shocking red hair. He was barely Hazel's height and seemed to be wearing an impressive collection of cardigans under a faded zoo maintenance jacket.

"Seems you've been locked on up in here with me and the beasties," he said cheerfully. "Let me guess, reptile house?"

Hazel gave him a suspicious look and stepped backwards slightly. Why would he know that? The old man gave a laugh like a shower of tiny bells and said, "Now, now, don't be afraid, I'm no devil. Nigel Hamstring, the blighter of a guard in charge of clearing the west buildings, he's about as scared of a snake as a mouse fears a cat! He never checks inside, prefers just to call into the building to see if anyone is left and then skives off for a cigarette out back. You wouldn't be the first to be missed in there by accident."

"Yes, just so," replied Hazel, devising a story in her head. Bec interrupted, "We were hiding in there, sir. Someone was following us, and we were scared and now we have no way out."

"Followed, were you? Well, that sounds a worry, I dare say. I can let you out the back gate, that's the way I come and go. Let me stow my kit and I'll get you to the street. I suppose you can find your way home from there?"

"Yes, certainly," replied Hazel, raising an eyebrow at Bec.

"I'll not be a moment," said the man and he shuffled along with his cart to a shed just along the path. He unlocked it and pulled the cart inside.

"Why did you tell him the truth?" Hazel whispered. "We can't trust everyone!"

"I don't know," replied Bec. "I just didn't like lying to him. I know we don't know what our enemies look like, or

69

what else might be out there, but I just get a good feeling about him. Can we try to trust him?"

"All right," said Hazel but she stayed on her guard as the little man came back from the shed.

"The name is Malcolm Duff Macanerny. Folks call me Duff though, so you may as might too."

"Pleasure to meet you," said Bec offering his hand to the man who shook it in response with a surprisingly firm grip. "I'm Bec, and this is my friend Hazel."

They followed Duff through a small gate, nearly hidden in a large shrub behind the camel pen. They came out onto a canal footpath and Duff led them along it to a little bridge. "The Regent's Canal," Duff said gesturing toward the water. "Seldom used and perhaps not the most savoury of places but here we go and up," he said in his funny trilling voice. The path led them over a footbridge and through a thicket and across another road until they emerged at the edge of the park.

"Out from the beasties and the London Zoo!" said Duff chuckling. "You all right now, kiddlings?"

"Yes, fine," said Hazel quickly. "We're fine from here."

"Right-o and away," said Duff, turning down the road with a wave.

"Thank you!" called Bec and then he turned to Hazel. "What now? It's too late for Paddington. Two people our age will definitely stand out lingering around a station all night."

They stood motionless on the pavement both trying to come up with a workable plan. They had been so carried along by the momentum of the flight from the Weever and the first clues of Joe that they hadn't really considered the more practical worries of being two teens alone in an unfamiliar London at night. Before they could make a move, they heard a gentle whistling from the direction Duff had walked and out of the shadow between streetlights, he appeared again. He had a parcel under his arm and was happily skipping a little as he whistled.

"Well, here's a fine pair of statues, Duffer old man," he said, seemly to himself, "not an inch budged. Feet stuck in the pavement, kiddlings?" he asked the children.

"Truth is, sir," said Bec, "we've missed our friends, it's too late to get home, and now we're not sure where to go until morning."

"Bother it is to be out in a night indeed. You come along with me and I'll have a patch of sofa for you if you'll take it."

"We couldn't—" Hazel began nervously but Bec interrupted, "Could we really? We could pay you something for the trouble."

"Do you intend to cause trouble?" asked Duff, eyes twinkling.

"Well no!" replied a startled Bec. "I mean…"

"Be still, kiddling, I'm pulling your nose. It's just across here," Duff said, walking toward a stately white house with a black iron fence. Hazel gaped first at the house and then at Duff – the two didn't seem to fit. "Round back," he continued. "Solicitor lives up in there," he said, pointing at the house as he opened a gate along the side. He walked across the drive, pointing at a small building that looked like a garage out the back. "I live there," he finished, gesturing to a little door in the gables of the garage roof. He climbed a rickety set of stairs and let them in.

"I'm really no more than a mouse and need not much and I do like the walk to work." He pulled aside a curtain over the room's one small window in the peaked roof. They could see a weathervane in the form of a giraffe above the mammal house right across the way.

Duff's house was no more than one room under the eaves. Though it was dark, and its furnishings worn, there was almost no word to describe it other than cheerful. Photos, mostly of animals, filled every free surface and drawings in bright pastel colours were tacked along the sloped ceilings. In one corner, open curtains revealed a neat little bed and a series of hooks where even more cardigans hung.

In the opposite corner, on top of a worn dresser, sat a remarkable cage. The intricately decorated enclosure was almost as large as the dresser and shaped something like the great Taj Mahal in India. The inside consisted of a web of crisscrossing ramps and miniature swings. Right in the middle was a small brown creature with large ears. It sat on a small swing and gently rocked back and forth using its long tail for momentum. It stared at them with what Hazel was certain was a sceptical look. Was scepticism possible in a mouse?

"Ah, you've spotted Newton. Pygmy possum he is. Rare," said Duff moving to the table.

"Oh dear," said Hazel, "the door on its cage is open." She moved toward the cage intending to latch the door.

"Wouldn't do," said Duff not turning around. "Newton has the run of my house, he does; just fancies his posh playground of an evening. Got it from the zoo. They had a rare canary in there for a trice but then the door broke and they couldn't bother themselves to fix it. Took it right from the bin."

"And Newton, did he come from the zoo?" asked Hazel.

"Nope, just showed up, he did," replied the old man without any sign that he thought that bizarre occurrence required an explanation. "Now what are your thoughts on a nice dinner? My thinking is that it's been more than a wink since you had a good chew." Duff clicked on a bulb over a small gas burner and pulled open the parcel he had carried home. "You go right on ahead and have a sit and I'll feed you up in a twinkle."

"We have some food in our packs, sir," started Hazel.

"It's Duff, girlie, and no purpose in munching on supplies when I've enough for half the zoo beasties right here," he replied, continuing to work in the small corner that served as a kitchen.

"Thank you," she said and sat on the soft old sofa and closed her eyes. Hazel knew that to trust a stranger just because he was being nice wasn't wise, but she had to agree with Bec, he simply radiated goodness and she began to lower her defences.

A moment later Hazel's eyes flew open as Bec shook her shoulder.

"You fell asleep, Haze, dinner's ready."

Duff handed her a plate and the fragrant steam wafted to her nose. Until that second, she hadn't realised just how hungry she was, nor could she say how much time had passed since the breakfast served by Kitty in the library. Was it an afternoon or days? Duff had fried up some steak and onions and the rich smell filled the little room. A soft white loaf of bread with crumbly cheese was set on the table along with a pitcher of water.

"Set to!" declared Duff and the Rangers began to eat. The meal was so good and they were so hungry that Hazel was hard pressed to remember her manners or even remember to breathe. Finally, with their plates licked clean and most of the bread and cheese gone, she looked up only to notice that Duff hadn't served himself a meal at all.

"Duff!" she exclaimed. "We've eaten all your supper!"

"Alas, I've got some strength left in my bones, but my gut has seen some years," he said, patting his belly. "I don't eat much these days. A glass of milk and a carrot sets me right."

"But you went to the market for beef!" Hazel gasped, changing from embarrassed to suspicious. "How did you know we'd still be standing on the pavement when you returned?"

"To be sure. I had to figure that a couple of Rangers would be needing a place to stay and would be carrying about some awfully good hunger."

Hazel leapt to her feet sending her plate and fork to the ground.

"Who are you?" Bec stammered, grabbing Hazel's wrist and backing with her towards the door.

"Calm your trousers, boy-o," soothed Duff, sitting back casually in his chair. "I'm no enemy of the Wards. Now, I have a yearning for a pipe, and I think I'll just indulge. You don't mind? It's a filthy habit if ever there was one, but I'm coming past ninety and more, you know, and I daresay nothing will kill me now other than dying!"

Duff laughed his musical laugh and reached into a drawer under the table to pull out a pipe, a packet of tobacco and matches and set to filling his pipe. It was a funny long one that curved down into a big bowl. Duff looked so ridiculous with his cardigans, pipe and shock of red hair that it was impossible to be scared.

"How did you know?" asked Bec relaxing his grip on Hazel.

"What do you know?" she asked.

"What a deal of questions," Duff responded after a long puff on his pipe. "Well, here it is. I was, myself, almost a Ranger," he began. The children looked at each other, eyes wide. Like so many things, they hadn't had time to ask what happened to Rangers when they grew up, but neither had exactly imagined them getting jobs at zoos and growing old.

"Almost?" asked Bec.

"Hold on up with the questions, boy-o, and let me get some things out of me first. A few or more years ago, I cannot figure exactly how many – maths are for the young – my sister Deirdre and I were taken in by Mrs. Withersnips. You see, our mum died and never knew Da. We travelled to Fairwarren and we were scared like nothing but we were none too sorry when we reached the house I'll say. We'd not seen anything that grand in all our days."

Bec and Hazel had ceased asking questions and sat in rapt attention listening to the old man's story. As they sat, Newton quietly leapt from the dresser to the sofa, alighting on Hazel's arm. She jumped just a bit but quickly focused back on Duff while the little creature settled happily on her shoulder.

"Well, you have seen the house and met them, the Wardens, so I'll not trouble you with the details of our arrival. Soon enough, Mrs. Withersnips began to teach us about the Wards and the Corridor. We spent a good many hours and days in that library reading about times that are, that might have been and that might arise. Downright head swirling, I'd say! We must've been there a good number of months when she told us, told us we were Rangers, needed over in the Wards. I'd say Deirdre was as chuffed as a person could be. Adventurer from the womb. Me, had some doubts I did, but I was never going to let Deirdre go hopping about between worlds alone, so I set about learning what I was meant to learn.

"Finally, we were called upon to go. Mr. Yi told us we needed to stop an event from occurring that threatened to shift two Wards farther apart. I'll tell you what, I will remember that day like it was yesterday for whatever moments I have left. We got down there, along the Corridor as you know, and Deirdre pointed out the door we needed. Did not seem like anything to me and when I went to the door, I couldn't open it. Not a smidge. Deirdre gave it a try and it swung open as easy as that." Duff snapped his fingers.

"I was more than a mite scared and told Deirdre we needed to go back and tell them what happened, but she was not to be put off of a thing. She told me I just needed to go with her and she would manage the doors. Didn't seem right but I could not see a path to convincing that sister. She took my hand but just as she was about to step through, we heard Mrs. Withersnips shouting from the end of the Corridor, 'Stop,' she did yell, 'it's a mistake. He's a mistake. We've made a dreadful error.' Words to chill my soul but I knew them as true. I felt it. Which is to say I felt nothing while my sister was all a buzz with the sense of her purpose.

"Mrs. Withersnips did keep on yelling 'He can't go through.' But Deirdre was a person of her own mind. She said to me, 'Malcolm, trust me brother, if you're with me you'll be safe. I have to go, it's calling me. I can fix it and you can stay with me.'

"I don't mind telling you kiddlings that I was a jitter through and through and all manner of confused as to what I should be doing. But that girl was my sister and with her I must stay. She took my hand and led me through."

Bec was almost falling off the sofa as he leaned in, hanging on every word. Hazel, no less drawn in, was listening so intently she hardly noticed that the little possum had curled its tail around her ear.

"I'll not tell much of that moment, friends. The pain of a thousand knives does not describe," Duff said sadly and he pushed up his many cardigans and shirt sleeve to reveal an arm so marred with a web of tiny scars, there seemed to be no skin remaining. "Covered my face with my arms the second I felt the pain, and glad of it too. Scars set folks on edge, I'm afraid, but mine can most be covered."

Bec groaned and sat back, covering his eyes.

"Be still, boy-o, hasn't caused me pain these seven decades or more. But you see that a journey betwixt Wards is not a place for a young one who is no Ranger. Where we emerged was here, in Two. Things in the Wards were calm then," Duff said. "So, me and Deirdre we were able to hide on up in a haven for a long while. I stayed in there and she went about and kept us fed and kept on about healing me. But that girl was all stirred up inside and she needed to go. Once my body was healed, I knew she would go and go she did. I stayed put, was not a way I could pass through again! Left on my own it all happened as it would. Was catched up and sent about to an orphanage. Didn't struggle much, did I? My body was near broken as was my heart. But I was luckier than some and a man did adopt me. Not as warm a fellow as you would like, but nor was he cruel. Needed help about his boatyard and help I could.

"Now then, the rest is just the life of a man seen plenty enough years. I did always keep an eye out, though, for folks that seemed like they might be Rangers and maybe to hear word of her, of Deirdre. Though I can't make it out myself, I figured a haven was about the zoo, I just get a sense, and so I've been staying on there for as long as I figured that out. Thought for a spot Deirdre might come on through again but I finally realised that was not going to be. She'd have grown up and out of being a Ranger long since."

"You've lived your whole life in a Ward not your own?" said Hazel, as a statement more than a question. "She never came back for you?"

"Been all right, it's been," said Duff with a sad smile. "Never had much of a home over there did I, except for those months at Fairwarren, and to tell the truth, no one ever accused Mrs. Withersnips of being over motherly, did they? I had to let Deirdre go, it was just the way of things."

Hazel stared with a look of anger on her face. To desert her brother, never to return, seemed beyond cruel and this from Duff's own flesh and blood. She wondered at him being so calm.

Bec, who had been staring at his hands, looked up. "Hold on a minute, you keep talking about Mrs. Withersnips and Mr. Yi, you must mean their grandparents or great-grandparents, mustn't you? How could you possibly know them? Why, they'd have to be well over a hundred!"

"Good sight more than that, I'd consider," replied Duff with a chuckle. "Now Mrs. Withersnips, seen reference to her full decades before Deirdre and I came. Mr. Yi, he was new-like then. Stone cold calm I'd say, but not altogether knowing what was what. Maybe he has changed? And Kitty, well you know that one has been in charge longer than I think have the moss and stones!" His tinkling laugh rang out at this statement.

"Kitty?" gasped Bec. "She's a Warden?"

"Of course she is!" Duff laughed again. "Did you take her for all mince and crumpets? Ha ha. She does rather go on about the food, doesn't she? Loves to eat and to feed and her victuals have a specialness about them, I bet you know. But no, she's the one that is running it all, the Wards would be in a spin without her!"

"But how can the Wardens be so old?" Bec asked.

"S'pose messing about in the Wards, connected to their energy in a funny way, does a thing to ageing. It's brought me a few extra years I imagine though I wasn't ever really one of them. I've lived well past what you would think around here…" His voice drifted off and he sounded sad. Bec was about to ask what he meant but Hazel interrupted, her mind still very much on Deirdre.

"Duff," said Hazel softly, trying to hide her disdain, "you don't know what happened to Deirdre?"

"Wee scamp!" scolded Duff coming toward Hazel. She felt embarrassed and a little nervous at his reaction and regretted bringing up his sister. Then she realised that he was talking to Newton who had migrated from her shoulder to her head and was gently chewing on her hair.

"It is past the time for sleeping," Duff declared, releasing Hazel from the possum's claws and tucking him back into his cage.

He shuffled to a cupboard at the side of the attic and pulled out two faded blankets and a pillow.

"Make what nests you can on sofa and floor, kiddlings, there's water in the basin there about and the loo is out back of the place. Mind the wiry cat who patrols it. No friend of man is he."

"We have so many questions!" protested Hazel, but when she turned around for support from Bec, she found him snoring lightly on the sofa.

"Thank you, Duff, for everything," she sighed, not wanting to miss the chance for answers, but afraid of pushing the old man too hard.

"It is I to thank you, Ranger. Many a year will pass between when I get a hint of the Wards. And never before have I actually spoken to a Ranger. Your visit is a welcome thing to me. Now, off to sleep with you," he said with a kind smile but a note of finality in his voice as he pulled the curtains shut. Before long, Hazel was surrounded by the soft rumble of Bec's breathing and the decidedly less peaceful growls of Duff's snores from behind the curtain.

She sighed and covered Bec with a blanket and made herself a bed on the floor of chair cushions and backpacks and tried to sleep.

NINE

The morning came with a steady rain pelting the attic windows. Hazel groaned as she shifted on the floor. She opened her eyes to see Bec looking sheepishly at her from the soft sofa.

"Sorry for falling asleep, Haze. You should have tossed me off onto the floor," he said rubbing his face.

"And why should you sleep down here?" she replied.

Hazel thought they had been through too much together for him to act chivalrously. The door opened and a soggy-looking Duff came in, hanging his coat on a peg.

"It'll not welcome you out there today," he stated and headed for the kitchen. "A bit of porridge seems the thing to me." He fussed about with a pot on his tiny stove. "Sleep well and done, did you?"

"Yes! Thank you," replied Hazel, a little too emphatically. She did not want the old man to feel badly for his accommodations and she was very grateful not to have spent the night out of doors.

"Duff, do you know anything about Joe or Anika, the other Rangers? We need to find them and we've no idea where to look," Bec asked.

"Well now, that's a muddle. I did have my eye on a lad of late who was ever popping in and out of that reptile house. You see, I can get a sense of a Ranger like I did with you two kiddlings, though I can't be sure of them. He was about that place where I suspected a haven and I thought a Ranger he might be, but I did not speak with him. I felt good and unwell that week, hadn't felt so poor like in many a time, until yesterday of course."

"I'm sorry!" said Hazel. "If we'd known you were unwell, we would never have imposed."

"None such thing," replied Duff. "It's the Weevers. Can't see them, you know, not a Ranger and never was one, but that's how they make me feel – sick, sick like you ate a bad peanut and you want nothing more than a spot of tea and a curl up. They can make you feel something fine, like you live in a dream, I am told. But me, they tie me up in knots. It went on and on, those days when the boy was about. Must've been a mean set of Weevers. Hope he didn't get caught."

"What do they do if they catch you?" Hazel asked, now fully awake and eager to learn all she could from Duff and to get the information that the Wardens had failed to provide.

"I can't tell you, girlie," shrugged Duff placing two steaming bowls of porridge on the table, each with a large pile of brown sugar on top. "I would, but you see we were only a way through our training, Deirdre and I, and we didn't get to that part; then Deirdre pulled me through and you know the rest. But we learned that the things are as sneaky as the day is long. Like a jellyfish, their tentacles reach far, and a wee sting will set you back."

Bec's eyes grew large with fear. Something about their writhing arms made his skin crawl and Duff's description did not help to comfort him.

"But I thought Eris created them? Was she around then too?"

"This is not a name I know. I did understand that for long times since there have been people who have harnessed the energy of the Wards to make creatures to do their bidding. May could this woman of yours have recruited these old beasties for her own purposes."

The Rangers fell silent, contemplating this information.

"I'm not a much help to you kiddlings but for the porridge and a hard floor," he gave a wink at Hazel, making her blush. Duff must have heard her tossing and turning all night. "But I have a thought of something that might be useful to you – because you seem to be out and about ranging with no aim."

He walked over to the wall above Newton's cage and pulled a drawing off a nail. Hazel hadn't noticed it before – but then there were so many drawings that there was no reason one would stand out. The sketch was made in charcoal and its dark lines and shadows showed a boy about their age. It was not a drawing of a happy face. His mouth was drawn tight and his sparkling eyes were cast to the side as if in suspicion.

"I made this of that boy, the one in the reptile house. Not to be saying it is spot on, nor do I know if he is the lad you need, but may it be a help. I have not many moments to rest working at the zoo but when I can, I make a sketch," he said, gesturing to his walls. "Keeps my mind on the wide worlds out there, and away from the little closeness of here."

"Joe?" mused Bec, taking the drawing from Duff. "Can't say it wouldn't be easier to find the fellow knowing what he looks like!"

"Can't know for certain, but keep your eyes and your mind bent on his field. That is how you will best know him," replied Duff.

"Can we keep this?" asked Bec gesturing to the drawing. "It's very, very good!"

"Nothing at all. Keep it and will it be of help to you," Duff said, pulling on his coat once again. "Off and away with me to the zoo or my dearies in the aviary will be missing me. Rain is letting up. Give it a half-hour and then be along your way. It's of no good to linger with Weevers on your scent. Come on by for a visit and a nosh with old Duff if ever you come through this Ward again."

Hazel, feeling unusually bold, ran across the attic and threw her arms around the old man. "You have been such a help and so kind. I think we'd have failed by now if it weren't for you."

"Doodles and noodles," tutted the old man. "Girlie, I can tell naught out there will easily beat you." He patted her hand and then gently released her, doffed his cap at Bec and shuffled out the door.

"We should get going," Hazel said, straightening up the sitting room and storing away the blankets. Bec cleaned their breakfast things and looked longingly around the small room. They took up their packs and headed for the door. It was only then that they saw a small leather bag hanging on the peg by the door, where Duff's coat had been. A note was pinned on the outside.

Kiddlings, was something for me to meet bright Rangers such as yourselves. Got little sense myself of such things but I can tell you are a powerful set. I do not feel right in my head not giving you some help along the way. Please take this. It could be of use. Hurry along and keep yourselves moving. Duff

"I wish we could stay," said Bec before reaching for the door. "He'll be out for the day. Maybe we could just stay and spend some more time reading the journal?"

"We mustn't," Hazel said, shaking her head. "If a Weever got the sense of us, we'd be stuck. Plus, that won't get us anywhere closer to finding Joe. We need to get Joe and Anika back to Fairwarren, and soon!" Hazel slung Duff's bag over her shoulder and reached for the door. "Would be nice to stay though, this place feels like home!"

The two Rangers walked silently away from Duff's through the wet streets for about ten minutes.

"So, we go to Paddington?" asked Bec.

"What other choice do we have?" Hazel shrugged. "I think I see an Underground stop ahead. Let's go there, faster than the bus." In the tube station they were relieved to find that their money worked, giving them one small thing they need not worry about.

When they emerged into Paddington station, Hazel and Bec both stopped and gaped. The station, with its enormous vaulted glass ceilings and dozens of tracks, was abuzz with the morning commuter traffic. It was a sea of people, luggage, and stalls selling all manner of products. When Bec last saw it, Paddington had been boarded up and largely emptied in anticipation of bombing raids and was only partially in use. It was a remarkably cheerful sight to see the place so alive. Bec nudged Hazel and pointed his chin at all the people.

"Mr. Yi did say that our Ward was the most powerful but he didn't say it was the best place to live! This looks so safe, and peaceful!"

Hazel nodded and not for the first time she wondered if their Ward was wrong about many things.

They began to wander slowly through the station, amazed at the clean, lively space but not really knowing how to look for Joe. After about an hour Bec began to grow sullen.

"We could wander this place forever, Haze. What is the chance of seeing a boy who once said he'd be here in a note left days ago? Duff's portrait is good, but we might not even recognise him if he was here," Bec sighed and leaned up against a looming steel pillar. "Maybe we should just get back to Fairwarren and get some real help and advice."

Hazel was trying to think of something encouraging to say, all the while fighting the same doubts when a girl, maybe a year or two older, called out from a few tracks away.

"Oy!" she shouted in a voice that could not have been mistaken for welcoming. "Ranger!" She pointed in their direction and began striding over. A few adults gave her a critical look, but no one intervened. As she emerged from the shadow of a vaulted overhead beam, Hazel could distinctly see some sort of a haze or shimmer around the girl, like waves of heat rising up off the pavement. She should have been elated to meet another Ranger, but the girl's determined and hostile face made Hazel recoil. For no reason, she was certain this was not Anika.

Hazel grabbed Bec's arm and pulled him away across the station.

"But she's a Ranger! One of us," Bec complained as he stumbled after her.

"I don't care for her look, Bec. We need to hide!" Hazel shouted at him as they began to run. They wove in and out of travellers, luggage and carts, trying to put distance between themselves and the pursuing girl. Looking back, Hazel saw that she had been joined by a boy her age who was built like a barrel. If they caught up, there would be little chance of getting away.

Hazel saw a group of children and she pulled Bec alongside them, putting at least twenty of the uniformed youngsters between themselves and the pursuing Rangers. She looked around wildly for a place to run but Bec found a solution first. He gestured and she immediately followed, dropping to the ground and sliding underneath a fruit cart. They eased backwards taking advantage of a number of large crates blocking them from view. They could see the shoes of the schoolchildren pass and behind were the slightly shimmery feet of the Rangers.

"Bollocks, Frank, you run like a house. You lost them!" snarled the large girl. She looked peculiar wearing a sailor-style dress and patent leather shoes that you'd expect on a much younger girl, and her curled hair and freckles did not match her sour expression. The boy, Frank, was blond and while not exactly fat he was as solid as a bull.

"Hey now. You saw them first. You could have warned me!" he huffed in a whiny voice.

"They'll turn up again. If they need a train or are looking for something they won't have gone far. We'll find them," she replied.

Bec and Hazel exchanged worried looks. When they saw the feet move away, they backed out from the cart and toward the rear wall. The exit was far away, along the other end of the platform area. They had no idea how long to wait, or if they could outlast the older children and slip away. And slip away to where? They edged along the wall and Hazel pointed to a corridor marked 'Lavatories' between a shoe repair shop and a newsagent.

Suddenly, a hand grabbed Hazel's arm. She almost let out a scream but when she looked up, she saw a face she recognised, frowning at her from under a low cap.

"Quick, follow me," he hissed.

She stopped struggling and followed the boy who hustled her down the hall. She pulled Bec along behind her.

About halfway down the hall the boy bent down and lifted an intricately decorated grate embedded in the wall. He gestured inside. Bec and Hazel exchanged brief concerned glances, but both knew they had little choice. Inside the grate was a short tunnel, high enough for them to crawl through, which opened into a small mechanical space filled with pipes. Under a large pipe they saw a folded blanket and a collection of items in a wooden box. There was just enough room for the three of them to sit without touching.

Hazel and Bec took off their packs and sat; the boy followed once the grate was back in place.

"Are you damn crazy!" he growled in an accent that wasn't English. "Were you planning on parading around Paddington until half the Greys and cops in London were on you?" He looked from face to face but directed the question at Hazel.

Bec narrowed his eyes at the boy, "We were looking for you, chum – assuming you're Joe," he snapped, trying very hard to sound tough.

"Well you found me and near got us all nabbed." He still seemed angry, but he continued more calmly, "Yi sent you?"

"Yes, they all did. Fairwarren is a mess. They sent us right into the Corridor with no training. You and Anika and that Obcasix thing may have caused another rift between the Wards; they think we might only have days before everything becomes unstable, and I mean everything!" Hazel explained.

Joe seemed to flinch, but Hazel couldn't tell if it was the urgency or the mention of his partner, who was clearly not with him.

Joe looked Hazel and Bec over sceptically. "So, really, no training?"

"Nope," Bec responded.

"None at all," added Hazel. "We were sent to the Corridor the morning after we arrived at Fairwarren!"

"Insanity!" Joe shouted and pounded on the floor with his fist. He then ran his fingers over his thick brown hair and rubbed his face, displacing some of the grime there. Hazel looked into the face that she could now clearly see. Joe had large brown eyes and an almost heart-shaped face. She thought that he would be handsome – if the scowling stopped.

"Wait a second," Joe said, "if you haven't had any training, how can you suppress your field?" He was staring intently at Hazel, making her blush.

"I can't suppress anything!" she said, only then noticing that he didn't have, or have much of, the shimmer she had seen on the two in the station.

"Well, I can see this one quite easily," he gestured to Bec. "But yours is almost invisible."

"This one is Bec," said Bec in an oddly superior manner Hazel had never heard.

She raised an eyebrow at him and then added, "He's Bec and I'm Hazel and I have no idea why you can't see my field, I hardly even know what that is."

Just then a scraping noise came from the leather satchel Duff had left for Hazel. She had meant to look inside on the Underground, but it was crowded and she had been distracted by the sights of a war-free London. She cautiously pulled the bag toward her while Joe picked up a piece of lumber from the corner. She pulled back the flap and a small pink nose emerged followed by two long-fingered paws and a small bundle of sleek brown fur. Joe raised his makeshift bat but Hazel exclaimed, "Newton!" as the little pygmy possum scampered up her arm and settled on her shoulder, long tail looping around her ear.

"So, you know this um, rat?" asked Joe settling back down.

"He belongs to our friend Duff. Duff was once… well, never was… but could have been a, oh never mind," said Bec awkwardly as he reached over to stroke the little animal. "He's a pygmy possum, not a rat."

Joe gave him a confused look but shrugged and looked

back at the small creature. Hazel dug in the bag and found a folded note, slightly chewed at the corners.

Kiddlings,

   Take Newton with you. He's handy in a pinch and will help with the Weevers. Far more useful to you than me, though I'll miss him. Don't think twice, he wouldn't have it any other way.

   Duff

"Handy with Weevers?" asked Joe.

Bec turned to Hazel. "Do you think Newton masks your field somehow?"

Hazel shrugged; she scooped up the little creature and passed him to Bec. Instantly his gentle glow flickered out and Hazel's sparked to life.

"Useful rodent!" said Joe, looking a little more impressed and a little less disgusted than he had before. But then he turned seriously back to the others. "Look, I don't have time to train you either, but we should probably talk. Can't do that now, though, I'm starving and I just can't think when I'm hungry. I'll see what I can find. You should stay here. Rat or no rat…"

"Possum," interrupted Hazel, taking Newton back and tucking him in the bag.

"Fine, possum or no, they've seen you and you are only a liability here." Joe moved toward the tunnel.

"Stay," said Hazel, opening her pack. "We have plenty." She pulled out three sandwiches wrapped in wax paper, apples and a small parcel of scones.

"Kitty?" asked Joe, eyes widening and a smile breaking out on this face.

"Mm-hmm," answered Bec, as he chomped down on a ham sandwich made with soft white bread and a lovely sharp cheese.

"Best part of being a Ranger," said Joe accepting one of the packages from Hazel.

The three ate in silence for a few minutes, but it did not take them long to finish and wipe the crumbs from their mouths. Joe leaned back against some mechanical equipment and belched.

"Pardon me, haven't had company in a long while. Now, where on earth to start?"

TEN

Joe was a lively storyteller and more than once he clobbered his head on an overhead pipe when he jumped up to demonstrate a point. They spoke of many things. First, Bec and Hazel updated Joe on the war in their own Ward and related their journeys to Fairwarren. Joe, in turn, explained that he was from New York and had been a Ranger for about a year.

"I ran away from a difficult foster family situation, if you get my meaning." He laughed as he said it but then shifted uncomfortably and focused his gaze on the sole of his boot. He suddenly felt aware that quite possibly neither of these nice English kids had any clue about his meaning.

Bec, however, shook his head slowly and said, "Pretty rough, I suppose." It was not a question. "Father took the strap to me quite often. I would have run away too if I had your bravery." Hazel looked over at Bec, her head cocked to one side. There was so much she didn't know about this boy she considered her best friend.

Joe nodded and continued, "Got a job in a diner near the waterfront doing dishes and running errands. I slept in a shed out back and thought I had it okay. Then one day, this funny man in a bowler hat comes in and orders key lime pie."

"Yi!" Bec interrupted, but Joe just carried on with a nod.

"It was late, and no other customers were there. I was in the front, scraping gum from the bottom of tables. Would knock your socks off to know how much gum is deposited under tables in a day! Well I'm from the City, right, so I've seen more than my share of oddity, but the sight of such a fellow in his waistcoat and monocle, Rolls parked out front, ordering a key lime pie, well that had the crew in titters. Fellow picked at that pie like it might turn around and bite him. Eventually, he came on over to where I was and put a coin in the jukebox. Played 'Chatanooga Choo Choo' by Glenn Miller. Funny choice really, but as soon as the music kicked in, he turned to me and said, 'Joseph, we can do better than this. Will you be so good as to come with me: There is work to be done and you are needed to do it.' Only a madman would leave their job and hop into a car with a strange man in a bowler hat but I'm that very madman; plus, it just felt completely right. Bonkers?"

Bec and Hazel exchanged glances but nodded for Joe to carry on and he worked his way through his story.

"Mr. Yi said that my grandfather called in a favour years before to provide schooling for me. Unfortunately, it had taken some time to locate me, but they were now prepared to send me to a boarding school in Canada. It all seemed

94

kind of unlikely. But, you know, he was dressed nicely, he was polite and had hired a very flash car to come and find me. Seemed a lot to do to lure a kid into slavery or something. Also, my grandpops had been about the only decent person in my family. Maybe the old fellow had indeed pulled a favour from a friend before he died.

"So, I decided to take my chances with this fellow. You know, he seemed so calm and steady, like I was in the presence of an ancient oak tree rather than a man who could not be more than forty or fifty. He even offered to go see Uncle Cy – the one I escaped in foster care – but I said, 'No way, maybe I'll just send a telegram at some point and let the bastard know I'm not coming back.' I maybe used a few other words too, if I remember right. Mr. Yi suggested I select my vocabulary more carefully when I met Mrs. Withersnips."

Hazel and Bec both chuckled at this.

"The trip to Fairwarren was kind of a blur. Mr. Yi barely spoke as we drove through the City and boarded a train to Toronto. I didn't pester the fellow much, 'cause the first-class cabin was pretty darn nice and there was so much to look at. I'd never been out of the City before and those towns, farms and forests in New York State were kind of amazing!"

"We had more reason to go with him than you did but I also found it peculiar to feel so comfortable with such an odd man," Bec said.

Joe nodded and seemed to be momentarily lost in those times.

"Well, I got to Fairwarren and met Anika and they told me… about everything. You probably know the rest. Of course, Yi's tale was all a lie but I forgot all about that once I got to Fairwarren."

Hazel wanted to stay and talk forever, learning all about Joe's experiences, but she knew they were pressed for time and thought it was peculiar that Joe hadn't mentioned why Anika was not with him.

"Joe," Hazel asked cautiously, "what about Anika? We were sent to find you both. I assume that is what you are doing as well, looking for her? We found your note in the Haven at London Zoo."

"Figured she'd never see it," Joe responded with a sigh. "Paddington was one of our safe spots. It's good to have ones that aren't Havens. You might have found that they are great for evading Weevers but they're a nuisance if they get unstable. I thought if I stayed here for a while, she'd be sure to come, but she hasn't, and now I have no choice but to go after her."

"Do you have any idea where we should look?" Hazel asked hopefully but given how much time Joe had waited here in Paddington, it didn't seem very likely that he had a plan.

"Not really. She was interested in some crazy ideas and I think she must have decided to try another Ward looking for information," Joe replied sadly.

"Without you?" Bec asked.

"Yeah, well, Anika wasn't so convinced I would support her and damn it, she was right. I didn't like her plans and we fought some. I feel like an idiot for it now but it's too late," he replied, slamming his fists onto his knees in frustration.

"What was she looking for?" Bec leaned in, eyes narrowed.

"Think we'll talk about that another time," Joe responded. "Right now we need to go back to Fairwarren and find another Ward door."

"Where is your door? East End?" he asked getting to his knees.

"Hospital, St. Thomas," replied Hazel but she put a hand on Joe's arm. "I think you better tell us who those Rangers are before we head out. Are they Eris's minions?"

"Minions?" Joe snorted. "Good word! They're Greys. Rangers like us, mostly, who are turned by Eris and her cause. She can be very persuasive, offering a world where the things that hurt you are gone and vulnerable kids like us have power. Often, she gets to Ranger candidates even before the Wardens do. Those are the scariest because they've only ever worked for her and thought her way. Greys like Bethany and Frank are brutes. I don't think they have a real connection to any Ward; they just see themselves as the right hand of Eris."

"So, in addition to mind-altering creatures of doom, we also have a couple of oversized evil teens on our heels," Bec groaned.

"Joe, have you seen Eris? Do you know what she would do with us if she caught us?" Hazel looked imploringly at the other boy, hoping he would have reassuring words.

"Um, I don't," Joe kicked at the ground in frustration. "All I know is that she wants to, needs to, rid the Wards of Rangers because we repair them and keep the balance. She can't splinter the Wards if we keep fixing them."

"Why would anyone willingly join someone who is trying to destroy worlds? It doesn't make sense!" exclaimed Hazel.

"Sure it does," replied Joe. "If you were a kid who came from no home or lost a home, like Anika or me, and you were shown a world where things were great and you were taken care of, wouldn't you want to stay?"

"Maybe, but she wants to fracture the Wards, not preserve them," Hazel protested.

"Eris promises happiness and harmony. That's what matters," Joe responded, growing frustrated.

"We can think about that more later, best be on our way," Bec soothed.

"Yeah fine, but we need to be careful," Joe reminded them. "I can negate my field, and Hazel has Newton, but Bec will be visible to the Greys and particularly to Weevers. I don't know whether they will still be watching the hospital but it's a pretty good shot that they will."

"Can't you teach me how to negate, or whatever that is?" asked Bec, sounding a little panicky.

"Come on, pal, I'm just a Ranger with a few months under my belt, I don't know how to teach that. Yi, that old so and so, told me I had a natural skill. I just sort of think about nothing and kaboom I'm just a regular handsome fellow with no shimmer!" Joe replied, his mirth returning.

"Emptying your mind comes easily does it?" muttered Bec under his breath. The airy and confident American got under his skin, though it was a little comforting to have someone with them who knew something, anything, about the Wards and being a Ranger.

"Maybe we should split up?" Bec asked, aware that he was a liability but very much hoping they would not agree.

"No!" cried Hazel, but then took a breath and responded

more calmly. "No. Remember the second rule? You aren't the very best with directions and what good will it do us to have you out there drawing the attention of the Weevers; we all need to get through the door together. We all go and just try to keep ahead of them. If you stay close, Newton's masking may help you a bit too."

The other two nodded and they began crawling toward the grate. Joe gestured for them to follow and they successfully exited the station undetected. Pausing alongside a police box, Joe looked around to decide which way to go.

"I know you've been skulking around here for a while, mate," said Bec, "but you aren't local, so I think we'd better handle the directions from here. The hospital is that way." Bec pointed to the left and then swung his finger back to the right and then straight ahead. He flushed as he tried to look decisive. Hazel nudged his arm until it was pointing back to the right and the trio started out.

"I think we'd better walk," Hazel said. "We ran into some trouble on a bus before. Not too many teens riding buses in the middle of the day I suppose."

For a time they felt safe enough walking south through the Bayswater neighbourhood amid the busy shopping streets and shining white facades. The day had cleared, and a crisp blue sky stretched over them as they entered Hyde Park. In fact, the rest of the walk to the hospital was so uneventful and pleasant, it was easy to forget the peril that faced them.

At length, the trio cautiously approached the ornate brick hospital. They saw no Greys and no sign of the Weevers but Bec nudged Hazel, pointing to the entrance where they saw the German doctor who had been so rude to them the previous day. Surely, thought Bec, the man would remember the children he had confronted and might cause some trouble. He gestured around the corner, away from the main entrance. An iron fence ringed the building, but down one side a gate stood ajar and a van was parked alongside it as linens were wheeled in.

"I bet we can slip in there while they load the carts," Bec said, and Joe gave him a companionable punch on the shoulder. Bec scowled but barely suppressed a small smile. The Rangers sauntered down the street endeavouring to look as if they belonged. As they passed the van, they could see a man in white dungarees pushing a heavy cart down the hallway within. Joe signalled to the right and they hurried in and turned to the side before the delivery man returned with his now-empty cart.

After trying a few doors, they found a stairwell and climbed to the first floor. The reception area was quiet; a few visitors sat on sofas by the windows and a patient in a wheelchair dozed by a potted fern. Hazel, Bec and Joe walked quickly past and hurried toward room 1255. Before they reached the room, a door marked 'Supplies' swung open and a hypnotic mass of tendrils curled out, extending toward them.

"Weee…" Bec yelped but the word caught in his throat as they ran down the hallway, shoes squeaking on the polished tile floor. As their destination grew closer, two figures emerged from the other end of the hall, faces bent with determination and malice. The Grey Rangers from Paddington Station! Bec's head swivelled from the Weever to the Rangers. "No," he moaned.

"Get them, Frank!" commanded Bethany, while barrelling toward them.

Hazel shuddered to a stop in front of room 1255 and pulled the handle. She could see the glow of the Wards pulsing behind the glass. It had to be the right door, so why was it locked?

"Curses," Hazel groaned.

She shook the doorknob again. They were trapped.

The massive form of Frank reached them. He thudded into Bec and pushed him back against the opposite wall with a grunt.

"Hell on earth!" exclaimed Joe as he too grabbed the doorknob and shook. Hazel looked up in time to throw out a leg, tripping Bethany who, unable to stop her momentum, fell forward and slid along the floor, hitting her head against a supply cabinet. Hazel shoved Joe to the side, grabbed a metal instrument tray off a trolley and hurled it into the glass – shattering it on impact. She reached inside to turn the handle and wrenched the door open.

Frank redirected his attack on Joe, throwing a punch that landed on Joe's shoulder, sending him stumbling across the passage.

"You devil!" cried Joe as he regained his footing.

Hazel tried to insert herself between the large boy and Joe before he could throw another punch, though all her instincts told her to get away from the beefy teen. Frank swatted at Hazel, catching her on the cheek with his large hand. The stinging pain caused her eyes to water. Then, still dizzy, her attention was drawn to the undulating form of the Weever, which seemed to be lingering, like a spectator, just outside the mêlée.

Joe launched at the large boy once again and managed to land a knee to the gut. As Frank buckled, Hazel pushed Joe through the open door and let out a relieved sigh as she saw him pass through.

The Weever, as if it had been waiting for the Grey Rangers to have a turn, ceased hovering and spread its form across the hall. The tentacles pulsed like the beat of a heart and its alluring silver hues shone in the light that peeked through the widow. The chill that raced up Hazel's spine was the only hint she had that this was not a welcoming angel. Almost in a trance, Hazel moved toward the creature, drawn in by its beauty and by a silent beckoning song that echoed in her ears. But as she drew closer, one snaking tentacle escaped the mass and moved toward Bec. The sight of that long, near-translucent appendage covered in a web of purple-blue veins shook Hazel from her trance. She drew away, bile rising in her throat, and she stumbled backwards.

Bec was struggling with the boy. The older boy should have the upper hand as he was both taller and heavier but Bec had managed to pin him in a bizarre-looking wrestling hold.

"Bec! Your hand!" Hazel shouted and reached for him.

Bec took it just as the Weever's tentacle reached him and wrapped around his ankle. Frank shrank away as the Weever closed in towards Bec, its tentacle trying to reel him in. Hazel pulled his arm with all her strength and though he moved toward her, Bec's face was contorted in a silent scream of pain. Then, his eyes glazed over.

Panic threatened to overtake her, but Hazel kicked out at Bethany who had begun to regain her footing. At the same time, driven by nothing but panic and unknown instinct, Hazel stretched her other palm toward the Weever, and shut her eyes in concentration. Warmth welled within her, starting as a tiny kernel and growing until it sprang from her palm in a flood of pulsing white light that crashed into the Weever. Its tentacle trembled, releasing Bec, and then dissipated like mist in a strong wind.

Momentarily frozen by what she had done, Hazel stared into the sunlit hall, as a glint of silver dust danced in the air.

"What the..." she heard Frank gasp from down the hall. She roused herself and pulled on Bec's arm again, thrusting him forward through the open door. She followed, grasping his hand as they went. The door slammed behind her.

Hazel felt the dull thud of Bec's landing in the Corridor and relaxed just a bit, her own foot hovering over the thick carpet. No contact came. In one impossibly short instant, Bec's hand slipped from hers and she was falling.

"Bec!" she screamed, as the air rushed from her lungs. In the empty space it seemed as if all that had come before was a long, wonderful and terrifying dream. Hazel began to lose connection with the shape and feeling of the world and wondered whether all of life was this endless fall into nothingness.

ELEVEN

The Corridor was noticeably still and quiet after the bedlam of the hospital. Only moments had passed since Hazel had pushed them through and Joe and Bec lay on the soft, worn carpet by the open door. Both boys were panting and dazed. Joe roused himself, went toward the door and called out, "Hazel! Hazel where are you?" He moved forward to peer into the mist, but the door slammed shut, leaving no sign of the pulsing light. He clutched the handle and pulled, but the door was as dead and cold as a tomb.

"Curses!" he fumed and kicked the door. "Will I lose them all?" he asked, mostly to himself. He turned to look at Bec who, rather than looking upset, was staring up at him with a quizzical and vaguely contented expression. Looking the boy over, Joe saw that Bec's left trouser leg was burnt off around the ankle. His skin beneath was raw and covered with what looked like thousands of pinprick-sized cuts.

"Damnation," Joe cursed again. "Weever!" He moved to Bec and reached down to help the other boy to his feet. Bec stumbled slightly as he put weight on his injured leg, but he showed no signs of pain. He just continued to look at Joe with a curious smile.

"Well your lordship," said Joe "we've managed to lose two girls, not a very good record for a couple of young men is it?"

"Girls," said Bec and he smiled dreamily as if approving of the idea.

"I need to get back in there but the Weever did a number on you and you are of no use to me like this. We'll get you to Kitty before I set out. Can you do a little walking for me?" enquired Joe looking worriedly at Bec's vacant eyes.

"Are you American?" Bec asked. "Because Americans are terribly swell. Do wish your President Roosevelt would come and help us out in the war though."

"I'll work on that," replied Joe and putting an arm around Bec's waist he tried to hurry them toward the main house. Just then, the floor rolled and swayed.

"Big oopsie in the Corridor," said Bec cheerfully. Then he frowned a little and added, "Mummy will be quite disappointed."

They finally reached the double doors and pushed them open. Joe felt as if he had returned from years away and he had almost forgotten how confusing this house was. He turned past the stairs toward, he hoped, the library. It was usually a good bet one of the Wardens would be there. In fact, when he pushed open the door, still supporting Bec, he found Mrs. Withersnips, Mr. Yi and Kitty all gripping the map table with white knuckles.

"Lord in heaven!" declared Kitty turning to look at the boys. "It's worse than we thought!"

The Wardens gathered around the two, pelting them with questions. Most of them Joe couldn't answer and all Bec could do was smile. He turned pleasantly to Mr. Yi and said, "I daresay I know you, small fellow." Mr. Yi arched his eyebrows and looked over the boy.

"How long did the Weever connect with him?" he asked Joe with a frown.

"I'm not sure as I was already through the door and had a poor view. It can't have been more than a few, maybe ten, seconds," Joe reported.

"Come along dear," said Kitty taking Bec's hand. "Why don't you give me some help as I fetch the tea things from the kitchen? Then we'll have a freshen up."

Bec nodded and smiled at the Warden, "Girls!" he said cheerfully.

Joe might once have complained that there had been an attack and that tea was not their first priority. But he had spent time enough in the house to know that what Kitty did, and more importantly what Kitty fed you, was not to be dismissed.

Mrs. Withersnips ushered Joe over to the sitting area and she and Mr. Yi sat across from him, eagerly leaning forward. Before they could start talking, another rolling shudder passed through the house, making the books hop on their shelves.

Mr. Yi began, "Anika?"

Joe shook his head. "I lost her, or rather, she left me," he said, head hanging down.

"And the Obcasix?" Mr. Yi asked darkly.

Again, Joe shook his head, beginning to feel the weight of his failure. "We were on to an idea of where it might go when Anika grew strange. She kept asking how it would help to install the Obcasix in the cradle. She said that the Wards were flawed, and wouldn't it be preferable to start over and get it right," Joe gulped. "I'm afraid Anika may have been influenced by Eris."

"All right," said Mr. Yi matter-of-factly, but his face was pinched with tension. "What about Hazel?"

"Hazel and Bec found me, but we decided we needed to go back to the Corridor and see if we could figure out where Anika might have gone. We were spotted at the door – Greys as well as a Weever. It was intense. I got through first, then I saw Hazel get Bec free and push him through. She was right there holding his hand but when she got through the exit, she just… disappeared. It was like she fell off the end of the earth."

Mr. Yi stared intently at Joe for a long moment and then said, "I believe that is exactly what she did."

"Was she wearing her pack?" asked Mrs. Withersnips as she idly picked sugar cubes off a tea plate and ate them.

"Well, yes, I suppose she was. What does her pack have to do with the ends of the earth?" Joe asked in an annoyed tone.

"It has everything to do with snacks, as Kitty would be sure to remind you!" retorted Mrs. Withersnips indignantly. "Is that all she had?"

"I think so," Joe replied, trying to picture Hazel in the hospital. "No wait, she's also carrying a leather satchel with a possum in it. It's called Newton."

"Satchel or possum?" asked Mrs. Withersnips. "Keep your dependent clauses clear, dear."

"Are you kidding?" asked Joe, looking exasperated. "Possum. And there's something else," Joe continued nervously. "When we were in the hospital, I mean at the door in the other Ward, and the Weever got to Bec, Hazel sort of lost it."

"What did she lose, dear? The possum?" asked Mrs. Withersnips genially.

"Not the possum!" Joe cried. "She lost control. She blasted the Weever with some sort of light from her hand. It was…" he hesitated, "like a weapon!"

Mrs. Withersnips's head snapped up to gape at Joe and then she turned to look at Mr. Yi.

"What is it?" asked Joe. "What's wrong with her?"

"What is wrong with Hazel is that she has fallen into Nether," responded Mrs. Withersnips. "What is right with Hazel is that she may be a Ward Maven."

"A what, where?" asked Bec, walking into the library with Kitty holding a large slice of cake wrapped in a serviette.

"Fascinating," Mrs. Withersnips interjected, ignoring Bec, "we haven't even read about Mavens in an age, have we Yi? Do we have that book? You know the one I mean. The one with the red cover and the funny illustration of the donkey."

"In my office," responded Mr. Yi. "I was reading it last week. It's a stag, not a donkey," he added.

"Yi!" cried Mrs. Withersnips. "How many times have we discussed the returning of items to the library?"

"WHAT ABOUT HAZEL?" interrupted Bec in a surprisingly booming voice.

The Wardens all turned back to the boy who quite clearly had his mind restored.

"Dear oh dear, volume!" tutted Mrs. Withersnips. "You better come and sit," she said gesturing to the armchair next to Joe.

"I don't want to sit," Bec protested. "I want to go and find Hazel. How do we get her out of there?"

"Might have let some memories slide, Kitty, don't you think?" chastised Mrs. Withersnips in what was meant to be a quiet voice. "Lad was rather more at ease with the Weever venom in him."

"Hush now, Philadenia," urged Kitty, "wee Rangers are listening."

"This is too insane!" shouted Bec again. "Hazel has fallen into some bottomless abyss and it's all cake and reading time here. What are we meant to do? And, I am not 'wee'!"

Mr. Yi eased Bec into a chair with a gentle hand, but one that the Ranger could not have resisted had he tried.

"There is much to explain, and little time to do it. Pay attention," he said, not unkindly but with a tone that strongly discouraged interruption. "When a Ward fractures, space is created between ours and the new one. But, the resulting Wards do not exist in stasis; they move and jostle, sometimes creating the impacts, or rifts, you and Hazel saw. When the Wards are near one another, you Rangers can step through. This is how you do your job. I believe what has occurred is that when Hazel used her blast to dispel the Weever it displaced the passing Ward. Joe made it across just before, and Bec in that very moment, but the space grew too wide so that when Hazel stepped through, she slipped into Nether."

Bec gave Joe a questioning look, which Joe returned with a shrug; he had never heard of Nether.

Mr. Yi continued patiently, "Nether is the space between Wards. It is a void. No one goes in intentionally and no one who has fallen has returned. However, it was Hazel's power that caused her to fall, and it is also that power that may be able to save her. Had one of you fallen, we would already be mourning you."

He took a deep breath and continued, "Ward Mavens have appeared on rare occasions. They are Rangers like you, but they enjoy a special connection with the Wards, allowing them to manipulate their movement in unique ways. They also tend to have special defences and power. We cannot tell you more than that at present. It has been an age since there has been a Ward Maven and we have a great deal to research."

Bec's mouth went dry. Everything that had happened since Mr. Yi took him away from Miss Crawford of Orillia made his head throb with confusion. There was almost no way to bring order to his thoughts. He had used a common door to visit a London with no war; he had fled and been attacked by beings that made his stomach turn while filling him with tantalising visions; he'd forgotten everything and then been cured by a cup of tea and the best slice of cake of his life; and he'd lost the best friend he'd ever had. Now, to finalise his confusion, he had just been told this friend was some sort of superhero – death ray, super-strength sort of things. He felt very, very small.

Mr. Yi continued, "There are several more issues at hand; you should hear them all. Joe and Anika were sent to find where a missing Obcasix was needed. As I explained, the Obcasix are a bit like anchors; they create stability for the fractured Wards. Occasionally, through accident or malice, the Obcasix are removed or displaced. Rangers have always been tasked with secreting them, maintaining them, replacing the missing, mending the broken. Without them the Wards are disturbed and unsettled, which is one of the reasons why we've felt the unrest here. Disturbance in the Wards radiates inward and concentrates here in our world. Particularly here at Fairwarren. Right now, we are all at terrible risk. An Obcasix has been displaced and two Rangers are missing. What is more, Hazel has manifested a very rare talent, one that suggests she may be more important than we knew. But this talent she has, this power, will likely get her in trouble as it is untrained and unknown to her."

Mrs. Withersnips shifted in her chair and let out a little snore.

"What are you saying?" asked Bec, head spinning.

Kitty approached the group from where she had been standing silently in the doorway. "What Mr. Yi has explained so clearly and in so delightfully few words is that this house and indeed all the Wards have never been in as much peril as they are right this moment," she said as she bustled around each of them handing out cups of hot chocolate.

"Damn it all!" shouted Joe, slamming his fist onto the windowsill, making the cup and saucer rattle.

"Language!" tutted Mrs. Withersnips from her chair, eyes still closed.

"Chocolate!" Kitty added and tottered over to mop the spill. "Drink up, lad. Made it myself so I am quite certain that it's perfect. Very restorative."

Earlier, Bec was a little sceptical about this seemingly flighty woman and her obsession with eating, but having felt the effects of her work down in the kitchen, he thought it unwise to refuse anything edible from Kitty. He caught Joe's eye and nodded for him to drink. Both boys did so and like a wave, the panic, fear and frustration they were both feeling about their friends washed away and were replaced by clarity of mind neither knew they could feel. It was wonderful. And delicious!

"Right, so what are we meant to do?" Bec asked with purpose.

Kitty and Yi looked at one another. "This has never happened before," Mr. Yi responded, "very little is known about Nether and there is no intentional access to it."

Bec felt anger welling again but the emotion seemed trapped beneath a layer of chocolate-induced calm. "So, I am meant to do nothing while my partner is simply gone?" he asked.

"No, not nothing," Mr. Yi replied, "there is much to be done. You need to assist Joe in the search for Anika. She has not fallen so far as Hazel, but her absence is a great problem within the Wards. She needs to be discovered. Further, the Obcasix must be secured and the three of you must return here. The imbalance caused by Anika and the Obcasix will make Nether more unstable and more dangerous. If Hazel is to have any luck finding her way back, it will require as much calm as we can provide."

"But I have been looking all over London!" Joe added. "I have no idea where she went."

"Poppycock!" answered Mrs. Withersnips who had stopped snoring and was quite awake. "My dear boy, I do not lightly accept denials or lies. Which one are you engaged in?" she asked with a hard edge.

Joe's eyes grew wide but he did not attempt to deny the claim.

"Joe?" asked Bec. "Do you know?"

Joe looked like an animal in a trap, scared and desperate. "I really don't know. I mean, I don't know where she is physically, but yes, I might know what she was trying to do when she left."

"You had better tell us then," said Mrs. Withersnips, "because you are going to need to follow her, and soon."

TWELVE

Joe took a deep breath.

"It started not long after we got to Two... Anika was so happy to be in a place where the war had never happened. We were in Paris for a while for a repair. Anika was almost giddy at its war-free transformation.

"I began to worry that she would want to stop the mission and try to get to Denmark, to her home. You warned us about that," Joe continued addressing the Wardens. "Warned us against the temptation to find a Ward that was more appealing than our own. But then things got worse. We found a haven inside St. Vincent Cemetery and we were hiding there from a close call with a Weever. When we came out, we found a mason chiselling a plaque in a grave marker. He wore a scarf over his mouth and when he saw us, he shouted and told us to get out. Anika pressed him to explain – of course she speaks French. She is so annoyingly talented!" Joe shook his head in frustration but with a warm smile. "He told us that something called the Red Death had poured through Paris and indeed through Europe and had only run its course the previous summer; almost half the population of Europe had perished. Worse than the Black Death in the 16th century and worse – far, far worse – than the war in our Ward so far."

"That explains it," said Bec quietly, his heart breaking at the thought. "A new plague. In London, in Two, the streets seemed so empty and the hospital eerily quiet. There just weren't enough people around. They were dead." He recalled Duff's allusion to people not living long there and it all began to make sense.

Joe nodded and continued, "Anika went sort of wild, she couldn't believe there was something worse than the War. I tried to calm her down, but I barely felt sane myself. Could every Ward be nothing but suffering and loss? Were we trying to stabilise a series of places each more miserable than the next? Our work started to seem pointless.

"We were headed back to London and Anika had the Obcasix, she always did. Sometimes I, well… lose things," Joe blushed and cleared his throat.

Mrs. Withersnips made a quiet tutting noise, which Joe ignored.

"We were in our usual spot in Paddington and she went out. I knew something wasn't right." Joe's shoulders slumped and his eyes began to glisten. He hung his head and stopped talking. Bec looked around at the Wardens expecting someone to step in to soothe the boy but no one did.

He walked over to Joe and put his hand on the other

boy's shoulder. "All right, chum, you couldn't have known. Why don't you finish telling us what happened?"

Joe sniffed and wiped his face on his sleeve.

"Manners!" chided Mrs. Withersnips who was still in her chair with her eyes closed. Bec couldn't help but think that it was quite inconvenient that Mrs. Withersnips's remarkable vision seemed to extend to breaches in etiquette but not to finding Rangers.

"I left notes at some of the usual spots. I waited at Paddington for days. Anika didn't come back. I didn't like to do it, but I went through her pack which she had left behind. I found this." Joe reached into his jacket and pulled out a small grey leaflet. Printed on the front in red capital letters were the words:

FREE, INDEPENDENT WARDS FOR ALL

"It tells how unnatural it is to contain the Wards; how they should be allowed to break free. It makes it sound like, well, like we're preserving something terrible!" Joe exclaimed, handing the volume to Mr. Yi.

"We had concerns that Eris was spreading these lies," Mr. Yi said, thumbing through the small booklet. "I wonder how she got the pamphlet to Anika."

"Wait a moment," Bec interrupted, "who would even believe Eris?"

"This is a fair question, Francis," replied Mr. Yi. "There aren't very many people who know of the Wards but there are communities of Wardens in each Ward as well as past, present or future Rangers. They are the most important because they would likely need to do the work of splitting the Wards if Eris finds the way. Ordinary people, however, do pose a risk as well. There are always those who are swayed by the promise of power in whatever form it takes and will follow Eris. If someone like Hitler learned about other Wards, he would most certainly become bent on trying to gain access. Imagine the resources he could muster if the Wards could be breached. Imagine the lives at risk!"

"But who exactly is Eris?" asked Bec, his voice growing tense.

Kitty walked over to Bec and handed him a cookie. She patted him on the arm as he took it.

"About seventy-five years ago the forces trying to destroy the Wards grew more powerful. We believe they recruited a young Ranger who was easily swayed by the potential of that power, though we aren't sure whom. Unbeknownst to the Wardens, it now seems that Ranger had similar abilities to those recently displayed by your friend. Very soon the Ranger passed out of the Wardens' sights and was not heard from again. It was a very difficult time here at Fairwarren and we had to lock down the Corridor for years and rebuild the safety measures. The Wards grew fragile while we prevented Rangers from using the doors. Three years passed when our Rangers never left these grounds."

"I assure you young men that housing a group of teens with no purpose and no place to go was not a delight!" Mrs. Withersnips made a distasteful face, which Kitty ignored.

"The damage from those times was healed and we heard nothing of the rogue Ranger. Many decades passed before word of Eris began to spread. Whether she is a twisted and warped evolution of that Ranger we do not know. But she has untold abilities that pose a danger to all."

"But Eris is a grownup, right? So she can't move through the Wards?" Bec enquired nervously.

"We don't exactly know what she can do. We do know she has both Rangers and creatures she controls who can go through, though the latter cannot reach this Ward," stated Kitty. "Protections are in place so she can't get into Fairwarren. It would be disastrous if that occurred."

"Are you certain she can't?" asked Bec.

"Certain," Kitty said matter-of-factly, and she began to clear the plates. Then, as if she had forgotten, she added. "Unless, of course, we're wrong."

It took a fair amount of coaxing to convince Joe and Bec to go to their rooms for some sleep after the stunning conversation. Bec argued that they should be watching the Corridor, patrolling in case Hazel should appear. Joe pushed to go back to Two and see if they could find any indication of where Anika might have gone.

"All must be addressed," Mr. Yi assured the boys, "but plans must be laid in advance."

"Exhaustion will serve no one," Kitty added.

"Blast!" protested Joe.

"Language!" repeated Mrs. Withersnips from her chair.

Joe quietly turned to Bec as they left the library, "Let's head to the Corridor now. They can't help us, can they? They are only stalling because they don't know what to do."

Bec looked nervously back toward the library door where he could hear the Wardens' voices in a continued low rumble of discussion, and then he nodded.

The boys turned back in the direction of the Corridor, but after a few minutes of walking Bec recognised the stairs to his room. Joe was looking similarly confused.

"Damned rats in a maze!" said the American boy, agitated.

They turned around and walked back past the library in the other direction only to find they were once again heading towards their own rooms. Before they could make another try, Joe yawned and stopped to steady himself against a small chair.

"Curses," he muttered under his breath. "I'm unforgivably tired. Really could use a kip to recuperate. You?" he asked Bec, only to see the other boy fully leaning against the wall, eyes closed.

"Didn't realise how tired I was," said Bec.

"Kitty!" Joe said with a snarl, but he was yawning at the same time, which took the venom from his voice. "She's got a way with that chocolate!"

They were again at the corner where Bec should climb up to his room and where Joe needed to go left.

Joe shrugged and said, "Catch you later," and stumbled away to his room, falling into bed within seconds.

Bec stopped to rest on a settee just outside the ballroom, where he remained until morning.

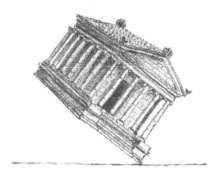

THIRTEEN

azel descended through the mist, losing all sense of time and space. After an unknowable period of time, she felt solid ground beneath her feet once again. The mist became darkness and she couldn't see her hand in front of her face. However, unlike the nothingness of her descent, she felt she was somewhere tangible. There was grit beneath her feet and the air had the dusty smell of an attic or garage.

Her first action was to reach for Duff's bag around her neck. Unclasping the flap she felt for, and found, the soft warmth of the pigmy possum. Newton squirmed and climbed her arm to take up his position on her shoulder.

"All right, Newton?" she asked into the darkness, scratching him on his head. Newton responded by curling his long tail around her ear. In this dark, strange place the little animal was deeply comforting.

Suddenly, the memory of the hospital flooded back in. Hazel felt her knees grow weak and her legs give way beneath her body. She sank to the dirt floor and heaved a deep sob that wracked her body. "I'm a monster," she groaned, thinking back to the Weever and what had come out of her body. "I'm a monster!" she cried again into the darkness.

Her beliefs and her sense of herself had been pushed to their limit these past days as she had learned about the Wards and being a Ranger. But this – this was too much. What was she? Without any way to answer her questions Hazel's violent tears eventually subsided into gentle weeping. She sat staring through the dark at her hands where something had erupted, turning her into a weapon. She was afraid for herself and for her new friends and she was terribly lonely.

Eventually, roused by the loss of feeling in her legs and a desire to figure out where she was, Hazel climbed to her feet. Arms outstretched, she moved forward until she touched the rough warmth of an unfinished wooden door. Steeling herself for what she would find, she felt for a doorknob and turned it.

Hazel blinked against the light outside and then inhaled a deep, trembling breath. She was most certainly not in the Corridor at Fairwarren. Instead of the endless hallway, softened by deep carpet and lined by doors, Hazel found herself on an empty city street like none she'd ever seen, or imagined. Though she emerged into daylight, there was something off about the light. Hazel grew up in England and was more than familiar with skies weighed down by cloud. This sky was not blanketed by coming rain, it was simply white as though someone had laid down a sheet of paper over the world; flat, cold and motionless. While the unnatural light drew her attention after the dark of the shed, she quickly moved her focus to the street in front of her.

She had emerged from a small shed but the building just down the street was another matter. Hazel had to crane her neck to see the top, but her mother would have been very disappointed if she had not recognised the fabled library from Alexandria, Egypt. Newton did a quick circuit of her shoulders and top of her head before making a sound distinctly like a whistle of awe.

Hazel tried to make sense of what lay before her. The Wards had each developed in their own ways but could there really be a version of the world where the Library of Alexandria still stood? And if so, did that mean she was in Egypt? She felt her heart begin to beat faster with rising panic.

Hazel turned and looked back into the shed. With the light from the street she was able to make out a run-down little room containing nothing more than some shelves with rusty cans and tools and a floor scattered with leaves. There was no sign of another door nor of how she arrived. Clear that she was not at Fairwarren nor in the hospital, Hazel had to assume that, somehow, she must have slipped sideways into another Ward.

Before she could consider it further her stomach lurched and a whoosh of air swept her hair over her face. Looking down the long street, she barely registered the peculiar collection of sights and buildings. Rather, her eyes were drawn to what looked like an enormous wave moving in her direction. But the wave was not a mass of churning ocean, it was comprised of the city street itself and all its buildings, undulating and rolling toward her. It looked as if the world were a table and someone had taken the end of the tablecloth and flicked it, sending ripples along its length. The problem was that this was a city, not a cloth, and Hazel was standing in its path.

Panicking, she struggled to gain control of her legs and began to run in the opposite direction. She ran past an Egyptian temple and what looked like a department store. Stealing a look over her shoulder, she saw that the wave was no farther than a street behind her.

Just then, Hazel passed an open doorway and noticed a thick black chain hanging from the ceiling. Vaguely hoping it might ring a bell and she could ask for help, Hazel took hold. She looked up to see the wave of city loom over her, throwing her into darkness. Hazel crushed herself against the wall, hand still gripping the chain, and screwed her eyes shut against the coming impact. Instead, she felt a gust of wind pass across her and a cold chill run up her spine. Hazel opened her eyes, which were wet with tears. The street was still, and she was unscathed.

Reaching for her bag, she checked on the little possum who appeared to have crawled back in and slept through the complete overturn of the world.

Hazel took stock of her surroundings once again. The doorway in which she stood was in an unremarkable yellow clapboard house. Adjacent to it loomed a large columned building glistening in white marble that looked like a small Parthenon. Turning back down the street the way she had come, Hazel's heart skipped a beat. The Alexandria Library was gone, as was the department store, and every other building she had passed!

"What on earth is this place?" she asked the empty street.

A Ward with waves that turned it upside down? She walked along the street trying to take in what she saw. The buildings were not lined up along the street as she would expect. Rather, each one seemed to have a completely different opinion about which way was up and which was down. In fact, the law of gravity seemed to be applied on a building-by-building basis.

The Greek temple was canted at a funny angle to the street, as if tipped up on one corner. Behind it, a red-brick building appeared to float high above the ground, bobbing lightly as if sailing on a calm sea. Hazel continued to wander, trying to make sense of this place.

Just then, Hazel felt a breeze and the vaguely familiar sensation of the ground moving. She looked around hoping to find a chain like the one she had found earlier. She had no way to know if it helped but the cool, dark metal in her hand had seemed to protect her. In the distance, Hazel could see the ominous swell rising and she dived down a side street at a sprint. She only looked up from the ground momentarily to get her bearings and what she saw froze her heart, and her feet. At least a half-dozen Weevers were swirling together over the form of a person.

The combination of attraction and repulsion overcame her as she looked upon the silvery forms. Hazel wanted to run but seeing the motionless form on the ground she felt a surge of rage and with it the warm, powerful sensation began to rise, unbidden, inside her.

"Oh!" Hazel gasped. She felt disgust and shame as the power surged more urgently. Accepting that she had no idea how to turn it off, whatever it was, she gritted her teeth and shouted, "Hey Weevers, over here!"

A few of the creatures shifted and seemed to look towards her. It was hard to tell – they had no apparent eyes – but Hazel had the sense of their pulsing cores leaning in her direction. She stood motionless, hoping the others would shift toward her. They did. The Weevers released the prone person and swarmed toward Hazel. She bolted back up the alley, heart racing, and turned onto the main road only just ahead of the cresting wave of city that surged behind. Sprinting as her legs and lungs burned, Hazel led the Weever pack ahead of the wave until, as she had hoped rather than believed, she saw a black chain hanging inside the entrance of a theatre. She leapt for it with one hand just as she felt the cold tingle of a Weever tentacle brush against her ankle.

She reeled back toward the Weevers, letting the strange light building in her hands break out. She shoved it toward the pack using her free hand, the white light shooting out as it had back in the hospital. The Weevers reeled, shrieking. They swirled in the air and retreated just in time for the wave to engulf them all. The great wave of earth passed through Hazel as if it were made of air.

FOURTEEN

Bec awoke, stiff and chilled on the hard settee. He stretched and yawned, beginning to recall all that the previous day had brought. It was not a cheerful recollection. He could not stop kicking himself for not sticking closer to Hazel. If he had beaten back that Grey Ranger when they passed through the door, surely he could have stopped her from slipping, or he could have gone with her wherever she went.

He continued to walk up and down the hall until, passing by the top of the main stairs, he smelled the enticing aromas of toast and bacon. Unable to ignore the grumbling in his belly, Bec hurried down the stairs to the dining room where he found Joe working his way through a substantial plate of breakfast foods. Bec scowled as Joe looked up.

"Relax pal," said Joe through a mouthful of eggs, "you were asleep and we're not going anywhere without a plan."

"Dear me what a sight!" exclaimed Mrs. Withersnips coming into the room with her usual shuffle and a bundle over her arm. She was glaring at Bec.

"I ask you, young man, what is the point of me maintaining a very decent little mansion here if you are going to sleep in corridors and ignore the very excellent toileting conveniences I have provided?" She thrust the bundle at Bec and he recognised some of the clothes from his room.

"Go to the adjoining parlour and make yourself presentable." She gave him a little push toward an open door next to the fireplace.

"You," she turned her attention to Joe, "I suppose this is the best we can hope for from you." Joe gave her a crooked smile. His hair seemed to stretch for the ceiling and he wore a leather jacket over a wrinkled shirt from the floor of his room. He also wore a knit vest and had his trousers tucked into his rough leather boots. He had declined to dress as Mrs. Withersnips expected enough times now not to be bothered and he knew the stiff lady was fond of him.

"At least, I discern, you have had the foresight to bathe. Irrevocable damage to the fabric of the universe is no reason to be slovenly. Oh, why must the girls always disappear?" she tutted.

Bec returned to the dining room, somewhat refreshed, just as Kitty walked in with her usual trolley. Atop were two sizeable paper bags.

"Oh Kitty, oh buddy old pal, you are a dream," Joe cooed, grabbing Kitty's hand and twirling her.

"We'll be on our way," stated Bec and tucked one of the bags into his pack. "Joe?" He looked at the other boy who was still busy trying to get Kitty to dance with him. "Joe!" Bec called again impatiently.

"Easy now, English, I'm coming." He grabbed his bag, planted a kiss on Kitty's cheek and darted out of the room ahead of Bec.

"A good amount of haste is in order," called Mrs. Withersnips as they passed into the foyer. "We need Anika and that Obcasix back!"

As the boys raced through the house toward the Corridor, Bec turned to Joe. "If there is such a rush, why didn't they let us go last night? And do they even know where the Obcasix goes when we get it back?" he panted.

"Not really. It's never been explained but it seems like these fellows have a way to look into the Wards and see where problems may be. I think they can see dark spots or shadows where there might be collisions or erosion in the Wards. They get an idea, but they never really know without us. Fool of a system if you ask me, damn it all!" Joe spat.

Though the boys were halfway through Fairwarren and had left Mrs. Withersnips behind in the foyer, Joe heard a stern voice from behind shouting, "Language!" He looked at Bec and rolled his eyes.

They reached the Corridor and opened its double doors. As always, the deep carpet and closed doors wound away ahead of them. There was no telling which door would lead them to Anika. They just had to walk until there was some indication of which one might be open to them. They walked side by side until Bec stopped, turning to stare at one door. It was utterly unremarkable, but the brass knob and frosted glass struck him as familiar. This was the door they had taken just days ago when it all began. What if this one gave him a way to find Hazel? He reached for the knob but before he could turn it, Joe jumped in front of him, placing his hand on Bec's.

"Pal, she won't be in there. Once you go through, the doors change; what's within alters every time. If you force open a door that isn't ready you could fall in and, well, there is absolutely no reason to think you'd survive that."

Bec sighed and nodded, dropping his hand and turning away. Joe gently guided him back along the Corridor and they resumed their quiet walk. About five minutes later Joe paused and said, "Well hello, beautiful!"

He had stopped in front of a large gold-plated door. The figure of a woman, half-clad in a gossamer Grecian-looking gown, ornamented the centre of the door. Her head was tilted down, but her eyes were cast up, beckoning them. Her arms were spread as if readying for an embrace. The tell-tale glow surrounded the doorway but the fancy door with the seductive woman made Bec uncomfortable.

"Are you sure there aren't things like trick doors? Something to lure us in a false direction or even trap us?" he asked nervously as Joe approached the knob.

"Never heard of such a thing; the Corridor is our buddy. This feels the same as all the other doors I've been through though I'm not going to pretend I don't like this one a little better," he winked at Bec. "No, English, I've got a swell feeling about this one. Ready?"

Bec nodded, and though he felt a little awkward, he took Joe's hand. He had no intention of ending up in some bizarre in-between place all alone. The surrounding mist came with the odd feeling of a vacuum and then they were through the door on the other side without anything sinister occurring.

Bec looked around but didn't see anything wildly unusual. They appeared to be in a rather smelly alley between two tall buildings. Joe walked up the alley and peeked around the end of the building. "Well I'll be a monkey's uncle!" he declared, skipping back and wrinkling his nose at the odorous dumpster against the wall. "I think we're in good old New York City!" he smiled. "My very own hometown."

"Really?" asked Bec, feeling somewhat better knowing the other boy was on familiar ground. "So, do you know where we are? Do you know somewhere we can go to look for Anika?"

"Don't get ahead of yourself, English. I recognise the sign at the corner, 45th Street. That's near 42nd and Broadway, theatre central. But this ain't any midtown I've ever seen. It's got all kinds of gadgets and gizmos and some crazy-tall buildings. A little future-ish, if you get my meaning?" Joe explained.

"The Wards don't change time so this can't be the future!" replied Bec, more to confirm for himself than to Joe.

"I'm aware, but this Ward is far more advanced than my 1940 New York! Actually, it reminds me of Futurama."

"Whatarama?" Bec asked edging toward the end of the dingy alley to take a look, while trying very hard not to touch anything.

"Futurama. It was an exhibit at the World's Fair in Queens last year. I got to go with Duke, the cook at the diner, before I left for Fairwarren. Pretty wild stuff they had in there with lots of models you could look at and walk through. Cars that drive themselves, stuff like that. What they thought the world might be like around 1960."

They rounded the corner and Bec stopped dead, mouth agape. They were standing at the intersection of two huge streets with buildings soaring up above them – so tall he couldn't see their tops. He'd seen pictures of the new Empire State and Chrysler Buildings in New York, but these were altogether different. The towers were made of glass and metal and lined the streets like a canyon as far as he could see; many were covered in movie screens flashing pictures in dizzying colour.

Bec pulled his eyes from the incredible city and asked, "If this is a completely different New York, how are we going to find Anika, if she is even here?"

"The door for this Ward would not have opened for us if there weren't something useful nearby. Now, the first thing we're going to need is a hotdog," Joe replied mysteriously and walked into the crowd moving along the sidewalk.

Bec had no idea what a hotdog was, and he could think of no earthly reason they would require a dog of any sort. However, he had established a theory that it was best just to go along with the American, so he followed close behind.

After almost half an hour of walking, looking at the soaring buildings, bright lights and sleek cars, Joe finally stopped and declared, "New York without hotdogs! What the hell is the point of that?" And he marched off again, his mood decidedly soured.

FIFTEEN

Looking around, Hazel took in the once again altered landscape. The theatre was gone, and she stood clutching the chain in the entrance of an empty chemist's shop. Across the street Hazel faced yet another disconcerting scene. She was looking up at the Coliseum of Rome – except that it was fully intact and not the archaeological site she knew from books. While part of her wanted to stay close to the chain, curiosity took hold and she moved tentatively across the street. Her nerves were strained as she was equally worried that she might come upon a gladiator as she was about finding more Weevers.

Passing through the narrow, arched entrance, Hazel emerged into the circular expanse of the Coliseum. The seats rose in endless tiers above her and colourful flags waved and snapped in a breeze she couldn't feel. While the Coliseum was absolutely still and silent, she could almost hear the roar of crowds and smell the thick odour of thousands of bodies and of blood. A chill rippled down her back before she focused her gaze on the most remarkable part of the scene.

In the centre of the arena a small Chinese pagoda hovered in the air, tilted at a steep angle. The cherry-red building looked as if it had simply stopped in the middle of being tossed by a tornado or, Hazel understood, by a giant earth wave. Other than the very obvious fact of it being in mid-air and tilted, it looked perfectly sound.

Hazel walked slowly around the arena, her shoes kicking up the fine yellow sand that covered the ground. She looked up at the pagoda, trying to make sense of its position.

"Always a bit of a mind scrambler," said a chirpy voice that seemed to come from above. Hazel looked up, shading her eyes against the bright white of the sky.

A face peered out of a window on the first floor. Hazel was surprised to see the round cheeks of a man with wild white hair.

"You aren't a Weever!" she exclaimed, not really meaning to say it out loud.

"Well I declare," said the man with a grin, "that is the most interesting thing I've heard in Nether in an age. Do, oh do, come up for tea."

"Well, I…" hesitated Hazel, both unsure of accepting an offer from a stranger as well as wondering how she would reach him even if she wanted to.

"It's not so difficult, just a hop up the stairs," he said, gesturing around the side of the pagoda. "I have a hunch you have some questions!" His voice sang out gaily as he nodded and gestured again to the far side of the building.

Hazel decided that after a dozen Weevers and the tsunamis, it was irrational to be too worried about a friendly old man in a tilted house. She walked around the building and came to the steps indicated. She tentatively put a foot on the lowest one wondering how she'd climb the slanting steps. But as soon as her foot left the ground, the house and its stairs appeared to right themselves and she found herself climbing the stairs naturally. Looking behind her, though, the rest of the Coliseum seemed to tilt unnervingly.

"Ho ho, no looking back," said the cheerful man from the door. "That'll give you the jitters. It's all a matter of perspective and you don't want to have two perspectives at once, now do you?"

Hazel frowned at the odd statement but reached out to take the man's outstretched hand. He was an unusual sight. His shock of white hair stood up from his head in a column and contrasted with his skin and his luminous sea-green eyes.

"Columbo Crimnus, at your service," he said, cheerfully shaking her hand.

"Delighted to meet you, Mr. Crimnus," said Hazel with a small curtsy. "I'm Hazel Benedict."

"Crimnus, if you will. I never could stand on too much ceremony," he replied, gesturing for Hazel to enter.

The little pagoda was so completely filled with objects it was impossible to tell the size or layout of the room. Hazel followed Crimnus through a maze of peculiarities. A bird cage hung from the ceiling upside down and appeared to be filled with feathers, but no bird. They passed a bicycle with no tires, a box of spectacles of a sort Hazel had never seen and a wall with four shelves lined with telephones. Hazel thought it was not all that different from Fairwarren, but the clutter gave the impression of a magpie nest rather than an eccentric estate.

Crimnus turned to look at her and sighed, "I know what you are thinking. I should have a good tidy! I know better than to keep gathering but I can't help myself. I really and truly can't." He stopped and offered Hazel a seat on an overturned oil drum topped with a zebra-striped cushion. Hazel sat as Crimnus fussed over a kettle and finally produced a cup and pot of tea.

"Here we go, here we go! A tea party at last!" Crimnus chirped. He bent to sit on an icebox and a button flew off his waistcoat. Only then did Hazel notice that he was wearing a purple satin waistcoat, white blouse and cravat and narrow plaid trousers – clothes that had to be at least sixty years old, or more.

"Blast these buttons!" exclaimed Crimnus. "I gather and gather and gather some more and still I can't find enough buttons. If I didn't know better, I'd think I was getting fat!"

Hazel stifled a chuckle by taking a sip of tea, which, she was unhappy to discover, tasted like sawdust. Crimnus followed suit but immediately spat out the brew. "Foul as foul can be! Got it off a brig, something to do with the Boston Tea Party, I think. Hasn't aged well, has it?" Hazel smiled shaking her head and put her cup down on the table.

"Crimnus?" she began but he stopped her.

"Let's have a game, a game in which I answer your first five questions without you asking. Ready?" he asked, eyes twinkling.

"All right," she responded. Hazel was beginning to think about the urgency of her mission, but her curiosity kept her quiet.

"One. You are in Nether. It lies between and around the Wards. It has no time of its own, no identity of its own. There is nothing inherently in Nether other than that which falls through from the Wards. This usually happens when there is a new fracture, a bump or a scrape between them. The sort of business the Wardens and Rangers are usually trying to prevent. How am I doing?" Crimnus asked enthusiastically.

Hazel nodded encouragingly.

"Two. You don't recognise many of the things and buildings here because they come from Wards you have not seen; Wards that can be utterly different than your own.

"Three. The space between the Wards is unstable. Every so often the whole place gets thrown on its head by the waves. I call them tsunamis."

Hazel held her breath. Crimnus had so far been more helpful than she could have hoped.

"Four. People can fall through. Doesn't happen much as people are more firmly tethered to their Wards than things. When they do arrive, they rarely recall where they came from. A blank and jumbled canvas, like Nether itself."

"That's very sad," Hazel remarked, thinking of the person the Weevers had attacked.

Crimnus nodded then continued, "Five. Chocolate with caramel and cookie."

"What?" Hazel asked.

"I see you looking at my Twix bar," he replied with a grin.

Hazel realised she had been staring at a small red package on the table near her cup.

"Go on, help yourself. They come from Eight, I think. Really very tickled when they come through, a favourite!"

"Oh, no, thank you. I couldn't eat your favourite chocolate," Hazel declined while noticing that she oddly wasn't the least bit hungry. "What is Eight?"

"Ah, a new Ranger!" Crimnus exclaimed. "The splintered Wards are numbered to keep track of them when possible. Not that we know them all…" his voice drifted off.

Just then there was a frantic chittering and scratching inside her satchel and the pink nose of Newton poked out. He sniffed the air, turned toward Crimnus and shrieked. He streaked out of the bag, over Hazel's lap, across the table and leaped onto Crimnus. Newton proceeded to run loops on and over the man, circling him in a frantic scurry Hazel thought would never end. Finally, the little creature stopped and settled on his shoulder, looping his tail around the man's ear.

"A pygmy possum is a remarkable creature you know," said Crimnus smiling down on the tiny animal and not looking surprised in the least. "Very few of earth's creatures can travel through the Wards. There's a deep-sea shrimp that can do it, but really what's the point? I'm also told the African white rhino has the talent but trying to get one of those through a door is nothing to sneeze at. So, your friend here is one of a very special breed. You've noticed his help evading Weevers?"

"Why yes! At least I think so, but there was a group of Weevers back in that alley that came after me even though

I was carrying him," Hazel mused aloud. "His name is Newton, by the way."

Hazel paused and thought about the Weevers attacking the girl before the tsunami and of the blank look in Bec's eyes back in the hospital. She asked, "What do the Weevers do to you exactly?"

"They feed themselves, if you will, by taking your reality and feeding you delusion. Their victims feel euphoria but deep down they know it isn't real and their own identity is lost. People end up sad, confused and unfocused. Not lovely company for a dinner party, I can tell you! The real trouble is if Weevers are allowed to continue to feed or they don't have enough food, they will suck away your entire memory."

Hazel shuddered and then asked, "Why haven't the Weevers gotten to you?"

"I happen to be one of the rare few that Weevers find very difficult to drain; I am a Warden you see," Crimnus replied, a little wearily.

Hazel's eyes flew open in surprise. *What on earth was a Warden doing here in this non-place?* Before Crimnus could continue, Hazel felt the now-familiar lurching sensation.

"Bother and drat!" exclaimed the Warden. "Hold on." Crimnus reached up and pulled two black chains down from the ceiling. The two sat at their tea table, arms outstretched, grabbing the anchor chains as the pagoda bucked and rolled as a wave passed over them.

"Nuisance really," Crimnus said when it was over. "I'd come to enjoy the view of the Coliseum," he walked over to a small window and, pulling aside a gold silken curtain, he surveyed the view. "Well now, won't complain about that!"

He leaned back so that Hazel could see outside. In place of the dusty arena, the pagoda sat firmly on the grass on a tiny island in the middle of a wandering serpentine lake. Up the grassy bank, a spectacular estate sprawled in the sun.

"Versailles, I should think," said Crimnus with a smile.

"Versailles? From France," Hazel gasped. "But why would that have fallen through?"

"Never easy to know why things fall but wouldn't Mrs. Withersnips be tickled. I do rather think she has a passion for the French!"

"Wait, you know Mrs. Withersnips?" Hazel cried.

"Well of course, not a very big group are Wardens. How is she doing? It's been a few years since I saw her. Let me think, seventy-seven it is now," Crimnus momentarily lost himself in thought.

"You've been away seventy-seven years? But why did you stay here?" Hazel asked. She recalled what Duff said about people not ageing around the Wards, so she no longer felt shocked at how long the Wardens had been at Fairwarren.

"Stuck," replied Crimnus who had gotten up and was puttering about his stove again, eventually pouring a different pot of tea. "As I am sure you know, the Wardens can't travel between Wards. I shouldn't have been in the Corridor at all but one of our Rangers was missing and things were very unstable, so I went to investigate. I found a door ajar. That is a very unusual thing. Very dangerous. I should have gone back for help, called on my partners and gathered some Rangers to help me investigate but I was arrogant. You know if someone – not a Ranger – tries to go through they rarely survive and those that do can be deeply damaged."

Hazel nodded, thinking of Duff.

"What you may not know is that while you can't pass through without risk to life, you can most certainly fall! Fall I did, though I almost felt as though I'd been pushed," he added in a sinister tone. "I suppose I spent many years trying to figure out how to stay alive and maybe how to leave, but eventually it became clear that this was home. The tsunamis are a headache but once you learn how to ride them out, they are utterly manageable."

Out of the blue, Hazel asked, "Crimnus, why am I a Ranger? I mean, were my parents? Did I inherit this?"

"Dear me no, I should think you would have noticed. No, Rangers are born when they are needed, and the ability has nothing to do with to whom they were born. In fact," Crimnus added softly, "many Rangers feel separate from their families, not entirely included. Some, I have seen, do not feel very loved. A parents' connection to their children is strong and they often miss this connection with a Ranger child, as if they can sense that the child belongs somewhere else."

Crimnus didn't ask Hazel if this was true for her, but the cloud that passed over her face revealed the truth of it. Her thoughts passed from her own parents to Bec's who made little effort to hide their disinterestedness. Maybe Bec would feel better if he understood that he didn't do anything to lose his parents' love, they just couldn't connect to him because of his purpose.

Crimnus seemed to notice the forlorn look on Hazel's face.

"My dear, why do we not begin to think about some rest? You know, there is no real night here, no discernible way to track the passage of time. I'm a bit of a traditional fellow and I suppose I did begin to feel that I wanted to impose some sort of time structure upon my existence here. A real treat when this great fellow came through!" He smiled and patted the side of the large grandfather clock in the corner.

"So, according to his time-keeping, it's nearing midnight and some sleep is in order. You will find, I think, that you aren't hungry?" Crimnus asked, moving to clear a pile of papers and debris from a very firm-looking settee near the clock.

Hazel nodded realising that she had been with Crimnus for many hours, and in Nether even longer, and hadn't felt the urge to eat, even with the temptation of chocolate.

"Essentially, time isn't passing here so your body hasn't really changed since the moment you arrived. Unless you arrived hungry, you probably aren't now."

Hazel looked curiously at the little man.

"In fact, you see before you the very vision of the dashing Warden who left Fairwarren seventy-seven years ago, by your reckoning. I sleep to avoid madness and I do indulge in an occasional meal, through habit mostly, and because eating is a delight! There was one time the tsunami dropped me right next to a charming Italian taverna, a few meals still hot on the table. Judging from the frescoes, I think it might have come from Pompeii. I ate a very nice pasta and grilled rabbit before it moved on!"

Hazel felt a shudder run through her as she contemplated so many years lived with no structure to the day, no change, no yearnings. It sounded dreadful. But here was Crimnus, seemingly content.

The silence was broken when the clock chimed. Hazel began to itch to move on.

"I'm sorry to be rude but I need to get back to Fairwarren, Bec will be worried after what happened and there is so much we still need to do."

Crimnus shook his head, "Dear girl, perhaps you have misunderstood. I wish I could tell you otherwise, but there is simply no way back from Nether. We are both stuck."

"No, that can't be!"

"My own tale should have convinced you."

Crimnus looked down at Hazel sadly, shaking his head.

"But there has to be something!" Hazel cried, her voice a high shriek. "I blasted those Weevers, twice, surely there is something I can do to leave!"

"Beg pardon?" Crimnus said, his voice growing tense. "Blasted?"

Hazel nodded; she'd had so many questions she hadn't even thought to tell Crimnus about what had happened. Hazel took a deep breath and relayed the narrow escape from the hospital and then what she had done again in the road.

"Maybe it was nothing, I know it sounds insane, but just maybe it could help?" Hazel's eyes shone with fear and hope.

"Oh my, oh my, oh my," muttered Crimnus as he hopped to his feet and scurried around the pagoda distractedly tossing items here and there.

"I may be wrong!" Hazel heard him say from the other room. "I may be right!" he added.

Crimnus emerged, looking ruffled with his hair whipped up in an unruly cloud.

"We only talked about it a few times, the other Wardens and I. Really more of a theory than reality. Didn't think it would happen…" Crimnus began to babble with excitement in his voice.

He walked to a short, lacquered cabinet inlaid with ornate gold designs in a Chinese style. He withdrew a small leather-bound book, which looked very similar to the Ranger journal, if a little better preserved.

"I have retained residence in this charming, but not very spacious, pagoda because I found it with this cabinet intact. I have a suspicion that our very own Mrs. Withersnips might have played some role in trying to get it through for me, though I've never been able to ask. This book relates some of the earliest history of the Wards and is really a dreadfully boring read. I have, of course, read it some 403 times but I can't really recommend it. It discusses many ways in which the Wards may become unstable, some that you have experienced. Some of the issues stem from the fact that the splintered Wards should be tended by a Ward Maven."

"A Ward what?" asked Hazel, feeling foolish for not knowing more.

"The Ward Mavens are a very rare subset of the Rangers. People who are intimately connected to the very fibre of the Wards. Their power can heal many issues that emerge from the movement of the Wards; they are the ultimate Ward keepers."

Hazel squirmed under Crimnus's gaze, not liking where this conversation seemed to be headed.

"If I am right, then it becomes extremely important – really utterly critical – that we get you back to Fairwarren without wasting another moment."

"If you are right about what?" Hazel pressed, starting to grow a little irritated.

"Well, that you are a Ward Maven, of course!" Crimnus replied.

"Me!" Hazel gasped. "Don't be silly, Crimnus. Sure, something funny happened with the Weevers, I know, but that is not the same as being some sort of all-powerful Ward fixer! It doesn't make sense!" Hazel protested once again.

"Make sense?" laughed Crimnus. "What about the last weeks of your life has made any sense?"

Hazel had to reflect on that for a moment. She realised that from the instant she saw the sky tear open over the Atlantic, nothing had actually made much sense, but she had gradually come to accept all of the madness as not only possible, but inevitable. Why should this be any different? She was not convinced that Crimnus knew what he was talking about or that she could even trust the eccentric man, but she did pay close attention to the part where he said they needed to get her back to Fairwarren. That, she couldn't agree with more.

"I thought you said there was no way back?" Hazel asked.

"Ah well, that is most certainly true for me and quite definitely true for a Ranger but not necessarily absolutely true for a Maven!" he responded excitedly.

"Well, how do I do it?" Hazel asked. She was picturing Dorothy in *The Wizard of Oz* from the movie she saw at the cinema the previous year. In the end, after many adventures, getting home was as easy as could be. She looked down at her scuffed and worn brown boots and chuckled a little. Probably she would not be getting home clicking those together. She saw Crimnus regarding her with a curious expression.

"I can't say just exactly how, but I have some ideas," Crimnus began to flip through his book.

SIXTEEN

Bec and Joe wandered the streets of New York for hours. The city was even more vast than the metropolis Joe knew from his youth.

As they rounded another corner, Bec noticed a faraway, worried look in Joe's usually determined eyes.

"All right?" he asked, unsure of how to talk to his new partner.

"Just don't know what she was thinking. Not sure I really know her at all. Anika is unique, you know. All blond and tightly wound. She's always on time and, if I'm honest, always in charge. A bit pushy really," Joe said but with a wistful smile. "I'm a Brooklyn kid, pretty much raised on the street. Nothing, I mean nothing, in common."

"But you like her?" Bec asked, and then regretted being so forward.

Joe laughed, "Yeah, I like her. But, in a pushy sister kind of way!" he added quickly.

"What do you really think happened with her?" Bec asked.

"The trouble started in Two, like I told the Wardens – with the Red Plague. Anika flew into a rage. She complained that there was nowhere to go in the Wards that didn't involve an endless waste of life and illustrate humanity's stupidity. I know what our job is, but she questioned it. She thought maybe the Wards should continue to break apart, like Eris says. It was scary."

Joe collapsed against a lamp post, shaking his head.

"Golly old bean, are you all right?" Bec asked, startled at Joe's new demeanour.

"Fine, I'm fine," Joe said, recovering himself. "I'm just worried about her, you know?"

"Yes, I know," responded Bec seriously. He did know. He felt so far away from Hazel and even though he knew that finding Anika and taking care of the Obcasix was the best they could do, he felt as if he'd abandoned his friend.

Joe nodded and got up, and the two boys walked on silently for a while, until Joe smirked and said, "Old bean? What are you, eighty?"

They continued on until they came to an opening between buildings and Joe gaped at the scene before them. Beyond the familiar gritty brick buildings with their rusty fire ladders and windows with peeling paint, the view of the city across the river was like a fantasy. The East River, which he had crossed over so many times at home, appeared not to consist of water, but of a solid forest of tiny windmills spinning in unison. Transparent tubes hung below the roadway of the bridges and draped along the side of rough brick buildings like strangling vines. Every few seconds a flash of colour signalled a train flying through the tube tunnels. Unlike the rattling and screeching subway trains he knew, these passed by silently. In fact, the entire city, despite its flashing lights, vast screens and sleek cars, was eerily quiet.

"Don't you wonder what happened to make this Ward spin off? What made this New York different from mine?"

In answer, Bec elbowed him and pointed to the side of a rubbish bin where a torn piece of paper was adhered with peeling tape. On it was a symbol, in red, that looked a little like the steering wheel of an old ship, a central circle with spokes radiating out and surrounded by a second circle. The words 'Separate Futures' were written on it.

"Bec!" Joe shouted. "It's Eris, it has to be. It has the same words as Anika's flyer." He reached into the pack and pulled out the leaflet. The same words and symbol were printed on the cover. At the bottom of the paper, in small writing, were the words '*Bowling Green, 10*'.

"Is it some sort of event, or meeting?" Bec asked.

"That's where we need to go!" Joe said and grinned broadly.

"Gosh, no!" Bec gasped. "We shouldn't go where Eris will be! Probably Grey Rangers and Weevers and who knows what else as well."

"And Anika!" exclaimed Joe. "She'd have to be interested if she is here. Either she is there trying to figure what is going on, or…" he faltered, "or, she's with them and we could bring her back." Joe's jaw was set in determination. Bec sighed; he wasn't going to be separated from another partner, but he was certain that this was an extremely hazardous idea.

"We have no clue when this is going to take place, or if

it already has. The poster could have been there for weeks, years even," Bec implored, knowing it was true but also knowing that he was looking for reasons not to go.

"True, but there's also a chance we might find something at Bowling Green. It's down the bottom of Manhattan. We should at least investigate. We'll keep our heads down and steer clear of Grey Rangers, OK? Stealth mission, I swear!" Joe was almost vibrating with excitement.

When they reached the small park at the tip of the island, Joe ushered Bec into a narrow alley between two buildings with a view of the green. It was eight and the streets were fairly empty. The tall buildings that loomed around the green were a combination of old brick and soaring glass structures. Far above, the shining train tubes crisscrossed the air.

The boys shared a meal from Kitty's supplies and took turns keeping an eye on the green. It was well past eleven before Bec finally spoke up, "I don't think it was tonight. There's nobody here."

"Yeah, I guess. But this is still our best hope. Let's find somewhere to sleep and we can figure out what to do tomorrow," Joe replied, clearly disappointed.

Bec scanned the storefronts in the adjacent buildings, noticing that one on their right looked empty. Dust and grime covered the windows and the storefront was covered in paper. He walked into an adjacent alley and located the service door to the building. Bec gave a good tug on the handle and was rewarded by the angry groan of rusted hinges.

Joe hurried to his side and gave him a punch on the shoulder. "Not bad for an old bean!" he teased and moved inside. There wasn't much to delight them inside the empty building but after a careful poke around, they found a worn-out office on the first floor. Its windows, grimy though they were, looked out over Bowling Green. A sagging leather sofa lay in one corner and a single worn chair remained behind the desk.

"Ideal!" shouted Joe, dropping into the rolling chair, which protested but held together. Joe propped his legs on the desk and leaned back in the chair. "Time for a kip!" he said and closed his eyes. Bec reluctantly settled onto the sofa and imagined his room at Fairwarren with the deep feather bed and a cup of warmed milk. Looking distastefully at the worn leather, he put his pack under his head and allowed sleep to take him.

SEVENTEEN

Crimnus closed the book he had been studying.

"What I can tell you is not much, but it is a place to start. According to *The Ward Codex*," he patted the volume on his lap, "there may be a key to opening a passage from Nether. I'm not sure whether only a Maven can find the key or only such a person can use it, but I do know that you have the best and only chance. The key lies in Westminster Abbey."

"What?!" exclaimed Hazel interrupting him. "But how is that possible?"

"The Abbey has been here a very long time, one of the earliest arrivals to Nether from the modern age. I am not absolutely certain which Ward it came from. I saw it once, it would have been over fifty years ago, but where it is now, I cannot say. You could try to search Nether, but you could wander forever. Instead, though it will sound crazy, you need to find your way to the Library of Alexandria."

"I've seen it!" exclaimed Hazel excitedly, then remembered that it was long gone, shuffled by at least half a dozen tsunamis.

"Alas, without knowing it, you were as close as you may ever be to a clue on how to leave. Inside the library there should be a map that can lead to Westminster," replied Crimnus.

"But how can there be a map in one place to another place that existed centuries after the library?" Hazel asked.

"My dear girl, Nether does not exist in time like your world. It has its own rules as our tsunamis should make clear."

"But it's all crazy. I need a map to find Westminster, but I don't have a map to find the library; I have no more hope of finding that building, do I?" asked Hazel.

"But that is where hope exists!" Crimnus beamed. "The Library at Alexandria has always been known for its towering spire, atop which the Flame of Knowledge is always lit. That light can sometimes be seen across the white skies of Nether. I have seen it on many occasions, though without any reason to follow it."

It wasn't much to go on, thought Hazel, and she began to despair once again.

A lurching feeling began and she lunged for an anchor. Hazel expected the usual sinking feeling and then calm and was caught off guard by the more powerful assault this tsunami brought. This time it almost felt as if a real wave hit the pagoda. The building and its contents rocked and shuddered and it was hard to keep hold of the chain. Hazel was tossed back and forth, crashing into both furniture and Crimnus.

When the crashing stopped, they tried to stand up only to find that the pagoda had come to rest at a steep angle. Unlike the first time Hazel climbed in, the building was genuinely off-kilter. Many of the furnishings had slipped into a pile in one corner. The birdcage had broken and the air was filled with downy feathers.

"Not good, not good, not good," fussed a rumpled-looking Crimnus as he tried to cross the room, but instead slid into a pile of silk robes. "All the time I've been here, never like this, not at all. Things are worse than I thought." He seemed to be muttering more to himself than to Hazel as he dug around the piles of oddities until he pulled out a telescope, almost as big as himself. Crimnus could barely lift it so Hazel came to his aid and together they managed to move it to the landing. He used an assortment of items from the newly formed heap to prop it into position on the sloped floor. Hazel watched as he twisted and turned the knobs and then, grunting, shifted the whole contraption so it faced another direction.

While she waited for Crimnus to find what he was looking for, Hazel took a moment to look at where the pagoda had landed. They were on a street with brick houses decorated with intricate iron balconies – flowering vines wrapping up their sides. As usual, everything was askew and acting without respect for gravity. Right above a particularly ornate house with a wide veranda, a small bandstand hung upside down. The colourful red, white and blue bunting that decorated it flapped about like a girl in petticoats who stopped mid-cartwheel.

"Bec would know where these buildings were from," she mused, mostly to herself.

"Eureka!" shouted Crimnus.

He eagerly pulled Hazel to the telescope and helped her position her eye to the scope. She could plainly see the tops of a dizzying array of buildings and landscapes, many disturbingly tilted or head over heels. She was about to ask what she was looking for when she saw it. The spire of the great towering library with a crimson beacon ablaze at the top.

"It's there!" exclaimed Hazel. "But wait, I can't get there from here, a tsunami will just move it while I'm on my way!"

"Correct!" stated Crimnus. "So I am afraid you must go now and go quickly. He slid down into the pagoda and rummaged around again and emerged with Hazel's pack and shoulder bag. Just then the pagoda shuddered and righted itself, the contents shifting and tumbling back into place.

"That's odd!" Crimnus mused to himself. "I'll have to look into that."

"But aren't you coming with me?" she asked, alarmed.

"I can't do that, there is no leaving Nether for me," he replied.

"But you said it was important, you said everything is at risk!" Hazel's voice was rising again – in anger and in fear. "How can you just send me away without helping?"

Hazel was shocked at the venom in her voice, but she was so tired of being sent off on impossible tasks alone while the adults stayed in comfort.

Crimnus hung his head pitifully, "I will help, if I can, but I can't go with you." He handed her the bags and then extracted, from an inner pocket, the small form of Newton.

"Oh, no," said Hazel sadly, the anger ebbing away at the sight of the tiny creature, "I can't take him, it's too dangerous, he should stay with you."

"A kind thought, child," said Crimnus with a sigh. "A little company would be nice, but Newton is a Ward traveller. He belongs on the move with you. If you doubt me, let him decide." Crimnus held out his arm. The little possum scurried in circles around Crimnus's arm, around his neck, over his head and with a twitch of his little nose against the man's ear he leapt over to Hazel, neatly tucking himself into the bag.

Hazel shouldered her pack and turned back to Crimnus, a look of defeat in her eyes. "I don't see how I'll make it there before the next wave and if I get caught on the way, I've no way of finding an anchor chain."

"This is where I can help," he reached into a crate on the floor and pulled out black chain. "For a long while, I have been working on developing this. It's a portable anchor. A shade of genius if I do say so. Loop it around anything sturdy you can find when you feel the wave coming. Should work as well as the others... should," he ended, with a little less confidence than Hazel would have liked.

"Thank you," said Hazel, still more than a little worried. She stuffed the chain into her pack. "But none of this helps with the fact that it must be dozens, if not hundreds, of miles away." She eyed the telescope and wondered how powerful it was; perhaps the Alexandria Library was on the other side of the planet!

"Not so far, I should think," said Crimnus. "And, I have something else that will help, if it is still in one piece."

He scrambled off the side of the pagoda and Hazel followed. To one side of the small building a rudimentary shed had been tacked on. Crimnus unlatched a door and scrambled inside. Moments later he emerged, pushing what looked a little like the motorcycle her neighbour once rode. He'd once given Hazel a lesson and a ride in the little sidecar. Hazel was pretty sure thirteen-year-olds weren't meant to drive them.

"It's fairly easy," Crimnus said, helping Hazel onto the saddle and flipping so many switches it made Hazel's head spin. "Press down on the foot pedal to go, the brake to stop and use the handlebars to turn like a bicycle. I've never taken it out for a spin so I think it should have a full tank. Just leave it running and don't bother with the rest."

Hazel didn't think it sounded easy at all, but it did sound similar to the ride she had enjoyed along the winding lanes of Buckinghamshire with Mr. Leslie eagerly giving her instructions. There was more to it than Crimnus had explained but she had a good memory for instructions.

"Now, if you go very fast in the direction you saw the tower, you have a chance to get there before the next wave. They generally don't often come more than once every three to five hours," Crimnus explained.

"But if I don't make it, I won't be able to find the library and I won't be able to find you again!" Hazel exclaimed.

Crimnus was silent for a long while as he looked out in the direction of the library.

"I have been here in Nether for more than six of your lifetimes. My existence here was of my own making and I accepted it long ago. But for you, Hazel, this is not the right place to end up. You are too young and there are too many things you need to achieve. Yes, you could be lost out there and we will likely not meet again, but the only way is forward. If you want a chance, you need to take it now."

Following the directions, Hazel engaged the pedals and got only a sad sputtering noise.

"Hopeless!" she growled at the motorcycle.

"Try again," said Crimnus encouragingly.

Hazel pressed again and was rewarded by a satisfying rumble. She took the handlebars and pressed the pedal forward with a resulting lurch. The next time she pressed more gently and the machine rolled forward slowly.

"Be off with you!" called Crimnus. "Be fast and keep your eyes open, the Weevers aren't the only oddity that has slipped into Nether! And, be careful who you trust!"

Hazel barely heard the last words, which sounded both mysterious and ominous, and for the hundredth time since stepping off the boat in Canada, she was struck by how little she understood about her new life.

She drove east keeping to whatever seemed like the most direct route with the most open roads. The initial fear of the motorcycle passed quickly as the sidecar made it easy to keep her balance and Hazel grew bolder. She pressed the pedal and revelled in the wind at her face. She drove on without event for a long time, the bizarre sights becoming oddly routine. Occasionally, Hazel noted something of particular interest to herself, including a circus tent, the flap open and the scent of animals and peanuts wafting over the breeze.

Turning to look at an old vessel, like a pirate ship, Hazel wasn't paying attention to the road. She looked up and shrieked and, just in time, she pressed her head to the handles, narrowly missing the vast ocean liner which steamed silently overhead. As the great black hull passed over her, Hazel turned to see the white letters on her bow proclaiming her to be the *HMS Titanic*. The great ship lurched a little to one side, rocked by an unseen wave, thus marking the sad end to a charming white clapboard church steeple off to the west.

Hazel's heart slammed against her chest at the near miss. There was something incredibly eerie about seeing the tragic, silent ship in one piece, cruising above Nether. If she had not seen and heard the very real collision with the poor little church, she might have believed it to be a ghost ship.

Directing her attention back to the road, Hazel was amazed to look ahead and see the blazing tower of the Library of Alexandria only a short drive away.

"I made it!" she shouted to the empty road. Elated, but still trembling with adrenalin, she pushed the bike forward at full speed. Hope was replaced instantly by terror as Hazel recognised that the feeling rippling through her wasn't just excitement – it was the lurch that came before a tsunami. The distortion of the road behind was distant but she couldn't have more than five minutes before it overtook her, throwing the library into some unknown location – perhaps never to be found again. She leaned into the motorcycle coaxing it to move faster.

Hazel looked back to check the progress of the tsunami but when she turned back to the road, she squeezed the brakes and the vehicle shuddered to a stop. In front of her, blocking the road, were five enormous lions, huge black manes framing hostile faces. They paced back and forth as if taking full stock of their foe. *Or was it prey?* Hazel's mind was racing. Were these the other dangers Crimnus was shouting about? She wished he had been more specific, man-eating cats seemed like something he could have mentioned. Looking at their sinister mouths, saliva leaking from the corners, Hazel decided that these lions definitely arrived in Nether hungry! Even as she wondered at their presence here, one of them let out a booming roar, which revealed a set of long, black forked tongues and multiple rows of razor-sharp teeth, like a shark. They weren't even normal lions from her Ward, Hazel thought, as adrenalin pumped through her.

"What do I do, what do I do?" rasped Hazel to herself, her mouth dry with fear.

The lurching feeling of the approaching tsunami was growing more powerful; the gates of the library lay ahead and the lion creatures seemed to have no concerns about the wave pressing their way. Hazel had no more time to think; she revved the cycle forward and threw the handles to the right, kicking up chunks of road as she turned. She drove the vehicle over the crest of the road and across a small stream. Accelerating right through a shabby wooden fence, she thanked her lucky stars that it was as poorly built as it looked. She continued around the side of a ratty barn and began to fly along a rutted path keeping the library in her sights. Three of the big cats leapt the stream in pursuit and were gaining. The other two had disappeared along the road.

Hazel drove on as her wheels began to shudder from the approaching wave. She aimed the motorcycle at the tall gates that surrounded the broad white steps to the library. Suddenly, one of the great cats leapt from the roof of a roadside petrol station and landed just to the side of the main gate, roaring and hissing at the same time, tongues lashing. At once, Hazel swerved and braked making the vehicle topple. She was thrown off in the direction of the gate, rolling painfully across the dry road.

Hazel shook her head and clutched her bruised arm. Scrambling backwards, like a crab, on her hands and feet, she tried to reach the fence as the wave loomed up behind the crouching cat. No longer thinking of the map or escape back to Fairwarren, Hazel now only hoped that the wave would not send her and the cats to the same place.

A rattling in her bag drew Hazel's attention and she looked down to see the flap pop open and Newton scramble out. Everything was moving too fast for her to grab him back. He leapt out of the bag, opened his tiny mouth and emitted a small squeal like the scream of a boiling kettle. The cat hunched its shoulders and cringed backwards, pawing at its ears. Newton continued to cry while Hazel groped in her pack and grabbed the anchor chain. She threw it around the closest bars of the library gate and grabbed hold. Hazel turned to see the large cats rear up, finally noticing the wave which hit them all with relentless force.

EIGHTEEN

A narrow shaft of light targeted Joe's right eye and demanded he wake. Groaning, he reached a hand up to block the insistent ray. He stirred and stretched his tight neck then peeked out through a clearing in the grimy window where the light had broken through and looked out over Bowling Green. He was shocked to see a fairly large gathering of people amassing around an ad-hoc podium set on the grass. Pulling the flyer out of Bec's bag, Joe realised that there had been no indication of whether the meeting might take place in the evening or morning. He and Bec had assumed it would be under the cover of night given that the topic was, well, evil. But of course, he considered, most people in New York would have no idea of the Wards or rifts or Eris and would not perceive this as anything more than an eccentric philosopher or politician spouting random opinions.

Joe was about to shake Bec awake when he saw a silver-blond head weaving through the crowd, its tight braids coiled on top.

"Anika!" Joe cried, jarring Bec awake. He jerked upright, yelping as his skin pulled free from the old leather sofa where it had adhered in a dried pool of drool. Joe managed to miss this one opportunity to tease him as he hurriedly explained that the meeting was taking place now, this morning, and Anika was amongst the crowd.

Bec hurried to the window and peered through the hole, trying to catch sight of the Ranger he had yet to meet, while Joe gathered their things and moved to the door.

"Joe!" Bec shouted as he turned from the window. "We can't just run out there. You see the shimmering? There must be loads of Grey Rangers, they might *all* be Greys actually! Plus, who is giving this speech? What if it's Eris? There are probably Weevers too! We need a plan."

"To hell with a plan," retorted Joe. "If we don't get out there, we could miss her."

"Joe," Bec spoke more quietly now, "remember the possibility that Anika doesn't want to be found. What if she's joined them? If you go out there rashly to confront her in the middle of that group, we're all dead."

With all his heart, Joe wanted to shout that there was no way Anika would do that, but everything that had happened before they parted made it clear that it was a real risk. Still, she was his partner and no matter what decisions she had made lately, he had to try to bring her back to Fairwarren. And, he had to retrieve the Obcasix and complete their task.

"Bec, you're a wise and thoughtful fellow," Joe said,

putting his arm around the other boy's shoulders. "Now wipe that spit off your face and let's put a plan in place that involves a lot of sneaking about!"

The boys searched the building as quickly as they could and were rewarded by finding a collection of dusty coveralls in a custodial closet. The navy suits weren't handsome, but they did fit in better in this Ward than their own clothes. Bec wasn't willing to leave the building without his pack so Joe insisted that he carry it inside a cleaning bucket from the same closet, to disguise it.

"What about the shimmery thingy?" Bec asked, looking down at his arms, still not really believing that he had an aura.

"For a walking library, you're not much with the words, are you?" Joe teased. "Probably we'll just blend in with the others." They pulled down the peaked caps and slipped out of the building the way they'd come in.

As they approached the crowd, the chatter died out until there was an eerie quiet for such a vast city. Joe looked up to see a woman of arresting beauty standing upon the podium. She wore the same muted clothes as the rest of the crowd but they hung over her tall frame as though they were an expensive gown. Her honey-coloured hair hung in waves over her shoulders and framed a pale, chiselled face that looked as if it might have been borrowed from a statue of an ancient Greek goddess. Her movements were graceful as she gestured towards the crowd. Her hands were sheathed in tight red leather gloves which drew Joe's eyes toward each movement.

"Comrades," she spoke at last, "we meet at the heart of this great city on a beautiful morning. But, do you not feel the darkness seeping in around you? The great forces of our universe are struggling against one another. The forces of freedom, of strength and of great potential are being torn asunder by narrow thinking and cowardliness."

Joe was barely able to follow the woman's speech, which could have easily been political or religious if you did not know about the Wards. The very sound of her voice was distracting and hypnotising as it poured out of her like molasses – sweet and rich – but with an edge of authority. Joe began to nod his head in unison with the crowd who stood silently mesmerised by her speech and by her slender red-gloved hands gesturing gracefully in the morning air.

By contrast, Bec barely heard the woman; he was mesmerised in an entirely different way. Watching the crowd, he caught sight of a girl about his own age. She had a long oval face with ice-blue piercing eyes looking out under slightly lowered lids. Her platinum hair was pulled tightly back away from her face. Bec's heart actually stumbled in his chest when her eyes cast over his. When the girl turned to look around the rest of the crowd, Bec saw the tight braids coiled around the back of her head and he realised he must be looking at Anika. His face flushed at the idea that he had been dazzled by Joe's partner. Just then, Joe managed to turn his head from the talking woman and caught sight of Bec.

"What's happened, fella?" he asked in a low voice, looking a little alarmed at Bec's reddened face. "You feel OK?"

"F-f-fine," stuttered Bec. "Is that your partner?" he asked, pointing to the blue-eyed girl.

"Hell yes," Joe gasped. "Let's go."

Bec reached out and grabbed Joe's arm, "Remember what we talked about. Go slowly. We don't want to cause a scene here. Too many enemies!"

Joe scowled but nodded and they continued to move around the quiet crowd in Anika's direction. They were only a few metres away when a boy across the green spoke to his companion and pointed in their direction and they both started to elbow their way over. Joe looked up in time to see the beautiful speaker's eyes shift in their direction, the deep brown flashing momentarily gold with an utterly malevolent light.

"Bec, faster!" growled Joe nudging Bec along. Just then, Anika took note of the commotion, seeing the Grey Rangers on the far side of the crowd moving hurriedly towards her. Then, she followed their path with her eyes and caught sight of Joe coming upon her.

"Fool!" she spat out at her partner.

"Anika, let's go!" gasped Joe reaching out for her. She shook him off trying to look forward like the other members of the crowd.

"Keep moving. You do not know me," she continued, her teeth clenched. But it was no use; Joe stood in front of her and she looked up to see the eyes of the speaker on her. Everything she had done these past days to blend in with the Grey Rangers and Eris's organisation was for nothing – thanks to the typically compulsive inclinations of her partner.

"Damnation!" she cried, ironically using one of his favourite curses. She took his hand and pulled him away from the crowd, north into the city.

"Joseph Hunt," she snapped as they ran, "if I try to lose you, it is because I wish to lose you. Do not try to find me!"

"That's no way to show a fella you love him!" Joe retorted, as he pulled Bec behind him. Bec stumbled as he tried to run with one arm grasped by Joe and the other pulling along his custodial bucket. As they headed north, away from Bowling Green, Bec looked back and saw the speaker. Her lovely face was contorted out of recognition and her gloved hands stretched out in front of her as if she was pushing something in their direction.

Bec, not paying attention to where they were going, stumbled and lost Joe's hand. As he recovered, he looked up again to see that just past the outer rim of the crowd two swirling forms were taking shape. Their mist-like composition made him think immediately of Weevers and his throat clenched in fear. But Weevers did not form. What did take shape was much, much worse.

On the trail of the three Rangers was a pair of unearthly creatures. They rose to the height of Great Danes with the heads of vipers; they ran with astonishing speed on six bent and hairy cockroach legs. Clicking insect wings lay back against their snake bodies, long tails whipping back and forth.

"Lord," was all Bec could squeak before his muscles came back into control and he sprinted up the street on Joe's heels. Anika turned and caught sight of their pursuers. "Iort!" she growled in a foreign tongue. "Skinths."

Joe and Bec exchanged panicked looks, not understanding either of the words she had just said.

"These creatures make her Weevers look like the teddy bears, yes? Understand?" Anika cried.

They all picked up their speed and hurried up Broadway. Though the terrifying creatures wove along the crowded pavement, bizarrely no one reacted in horror.

"New Yorkers hate cockroaches," panted Joe. "How is everyone not totally horrified?"

He didn't get an answer. Over his shoulder he saw one of the things flutter, its wings making a scraping noise that made Joe's skin scrawl. Flying cockroaches were a horror of his young life in his run-down Brooklyn home. Their hairy legs and oily-looking wings disgusted him as did the crunch when you killed one. But even as a boy he knew they couldn't actually hurt him. This thing, with its serpent head and dagger-like teeth, was clearly a real danger. It fluttered and lurched upward, launched itself off the wall of a building and landed back on the pavement a half block away.

"Ahead!" shouted Anika as she made a sharp turn down Wall Street. Against one building a rickety newsstand stood incongruous and empty. It was clearly from another time and would have looked outdated even in Joe's New York.

Haven, thought Bec, as Anika slammed through the tiny door on the side of the stand with Joe at her heels. Bec leapt to follow but his bucket slammed into the door frame and sent him backwards. As he scrambled to his feet, trying to extract his pack from the bucket, he almost missed seeing a Skinth launch itself at him – mouth agape and fangs dripping. Bec pushed himself backward into the door and swung upward with the now-empty bucket. He caught the creature under the chin, slamming its head backwards – it fell onto its back, hairy legs twitching in the air. Joe appeared from the shed, grabbed the bucket and swung it down on the creature with a sickening crunch. Anika caught both boys by their collars and pulled them backwards into the tiny room and slammed the door.

They fell into a pile as Anika looked down on them.

"Idiots!" she cried and turned away.

NINETEEN

Hazel shook herself awake, aware of a faint scraping on her face. She carefully opened her eyes and tried to focus on where she was. This proved impossible as her view was blocked by a tiny pink nose and large black eyes peering into her own from her cheek.

"Newton," she whispered, recalling the possum's cry which had miraculously stayed the lions. "You are a very extraordinary marsupial – you saved us!" Then she wondered if talking to a possum meant she'd actually gone mad.

She glanced around for the motorcycle but found it absent – swept away with the lions. She tried to sit up but it was difficult with the little creature on her face. Newton raised a tiny paw, patted her on the nose and then scampered down her neck and shoulder and into his pouch.

Hazel looked around and was elated to see that she was connected to the library's fence and the white tower still loomed above. Otherwise, she felt that her surroundings were not very promising. The dusty, shack-lined street she'd left had been replaced by a sprawling desert; low hills and craggy cliffs unfolded endlessly around her. But even more bleak, this landscape appeared to be almost devoid of colour. Hazel was reminded again of the *Wizard of Oz* when Dorothy steps out into Oz and the amazing technicolour world blossomed in front of her. Although this was exactly the opposite, as if the last wave had washed away every living thing's colour and left behind only a grey landscape and the white tower behind them.

Hazel stood and pushed open the tall iron gates, thankful that they were unlocked, and climbed the vast white steps leading to the entrance. A pair of dark wooden doors inlaid with gold loomed overhead. A smaller door, about her size, was cut out of the larger set and stood ajar. She pushed it open and stepped inside. The sight inside stopped her in her tracks. Despite the grey outside, inside the library light streamed in through high oculus windows causing beams of light to dance across an enormous colourful space. Soaring, fluted columns adorned with painted carvings of Egyptian faces ran in pairs down a vast chamber. At least fifty columns supported an ornately carved, beamed ceiling. Between each of the outer columns, tall shelves lined the walls, each one holding thousands of scrolls.

I'm supposed to find one map in all of this?

Crimnus was able to give her very little information about how to find what she was looking for once she arrived. It had seemed as if the most important thing was to traverse Nether before a wave hid the library. Now she was here, Hazel realised it could be an eternity before she was able to find a single map – even if she knew what it looked like. Again, the despair she felt in the pagoda threatened to overwhelm her.

"How may I assist you?" said a smooth voice from the shadows.

Hazel flinched and spun around. Into the light emerged a very handsome man in his thirties wearing a trim grey suit and a straw fedora.

"I am Dr. Amenei Seddik, the librarian in charge here. It would be my honour to assist you."

"You," stammered Hazel, trying to process the presence of this man, "you work here?"

Dr. Seddik nodded gravely. "The librarians of Alexandria are sworn to support the acquisition of knowledge for all who seek it."

Hazel smiled; she found this handsome gentleman calming and reassuring but she heard Crimnus in her head, cautioning her not to trust just anyone.

"How can I be sure you do not mean me harm?" she asked, hoping that she'd be able to make some sort of judgement from his answer.

"It is difficult to know whom to trust. Unfortunately, I have no way to answer that for you. I serve all who arrive here. Those that would seek to protect the Wards, and those that would seek to destroy them. But then I ask you, how am I to know that you mean me no harm?" He smiled pleasantly.

Hazel shrugged. She could hardly be a threat to this man, but it was a fair question.

"I am looking for a map," Hazel said, knowing she had no other choice than to ask this man for help.

Dr. Seddik did not respond but merely looked at Hazel with the same steady gaze and pleasant expression on his face.

"A map to Westminster Abbey. In Nether," she added.

"As I suspected, seeker of the Key," Dr. Seddik nodded. "This search is both easy and difficult. I can guide you to the chamber of maps but there I can no longer assist you. I cannot access the map to the Key. Perhaps you can, perhaps you cannot, but it will be up to you once in the chamber."

Hazel groaned as she understood that, once again, she was going to get only half answers and more mystery. She had no idea what the Key was, but she had grown used to the frustrating limits and the ambiguous answers of the grownups she met. She nodded and Dr. Seddik gestured for her to follow. They passed under the soaring skylights and along endless stacks of scrolls. "Dr. Seddik," Hazel questioned, "surely the library of Alexandria only contains scrolls from ancient times. How would it have a map to a building that was only constructed in the last thousand years?"

Dr. Seddik made a pleasant ringing noise in the back of his throat that Hazel took to be a laugh. "Knowledge has always been drawn to this place, throughout time. If it is known, it dwells here."

Hazel moved on to a more practical question, "If I find the map, can I check it out?"

"Now that is a most prudent enquiry!" Dr. Seddik beamed. "Indeed you cannot. Our lending library is on the first floor and is, I am afraid, restricted to popular fiction and periodicals. If you were to try to leave the library with a research document such as the one you seek, you would find that both you and the document come to harm. Important to maintain the integrity of the collection, I am sure you understand."

Hazel nodded, disappointed. She had to hope that the map wasn't too complicated to copy.

"You may, of course, take notes," smiled the librarian as he stopped in front of a set of bronze doors. He hesitated a moment and the doors slid open revealing a small closet. Hazel stopped and backed up, craning her head upward.

"A lift!" she exclaimed.

"Certainly," replied Dr. Seddik showing them inside. "I am deeply ashamed to say that there was a time when the upper reaches of the library were made accessible by slaves. A dreadful number of stairs, you know. But in time, this upgrade was made to the relief of all. I am not ashamed to admit that many of the librarians shared a cake and a touch of claret to celebrate." Another melodic chuckle brought a smile to Hazel's lips. The walls of the lift shimmered in a highly polished metal. The reflection showed Hazel a face smeared with dirt and hair a tousled mess. She felt slightly self-conscious in the company of such a neat and handsome man. Dr. Seddik noticed Hazel rubbing at her cheeks and passed her a crisp handkerchief.

"Nether is an unsettling place," he said with a smile.

At long last the lift came to a halt and the door slid open with a satisfying purr. The room they entered was breathtaking. A domed ceiling soared above them at the apex of which rose, Hazel assumed, the great flame tower. The room itself, a perfect circle, was lined with deep blue stone walls veined with swirling white. The room reminded Hazel of the library at Fairwarren, but infinitely grander.

"It's wonderful!" exclaimed Hazel.

"I have always found it so," agreed the librarian, leading them to a large round table in the middle of the chamber. "Sadly, I must take my leave of you. You must search on your own, though I hope for your success. Perhaps you will find a way to locate your map, I do not know. Please respect the rules of the library. Handle documents with care by wearing the gloves you find here," he gestured to an open wooden box containing sets of neatly folded white linen gloves. "No eating in the library and keep your voice down so as not to disturb the other scholars."

Hazel raised her eyebrows in confusion. "Ha ha," laughed the handsome librarian, his face lighting up as though he had shared the most delightful joke. "It is a little library humour. I don't mind telling you that you are the first visitor I have had these two hundred of your years."

Hazel now knew enough of Nether not to be shocked.

"Very good luck to you," said Dr. Seddik with a slight bow and he turned to leave.

"But how will I find you when it is time to go?" asked Hazel, looking up, but the man was gone.

Hazel sighed. Without any better ideas, she took off her pack and Newton's case and began to walk in a circle around the room. Her walk took on a rhythmic quality as she took a step, turned to look at the scrolls, took another step and so on. She found as she moved anticlockwise around the room, a slight buzzing sensation began in her ears. As she stooped to look at a scroll in a beautifully carved jade canister, Hazel dropped the handkerchief the librarian had given her. Stooping to pick it up she sucked in her breath.

Looking down at the lace on the edge of the handkerchief Hazel saw the letters CCCV XX woven into the cloth. It looked like Roman numerals, three hundred and five, and twenty, she believed. She wondered excitedly if it related to a filing system and she ran around the shelves again, now noticing small carved plaques next to the shelves with similar numbers. She followed them around looking for the 'three hundreds'.

When she had rounded the whole floor Hazel looked up, deciding it must be on the next level. She climbed the winding metal stairs and alighted at the top where she had a sweeping view of the stunning blue-hued library. Hazel raced around looking for the numbers; she found the 'two hundreds' and the 'four hundreds' but nothing lay between them. She frowned, confused and discouraged. The low hum buzzed urgently in her stomach, making her feel certain this was the right place. She backed away and then returned to the missing shelf location. This time, a pulsing orange light appeared in front of her. Hazel backed away and the light disappeared. She repeated the process and then approached even closer. The pulsing light grew stronger and flashed, causing Hazel to cover her eyes. Looking up, she saw that the shelves in front of her now bore numbers in the three hundreds. Excitedly, she began to search for three hundred and five point twenty. The scrolls weren't obviously labelled on their cases the way books were at the local library. Even though she was close, Hazel began to fear she would have to open every canister in the section to find the right one.

Hazel began to run her fingers over the caps that sealed the scroll tubes. Some were simple wood circles like the lid to a lotion jar, but others were intricately carved in ivory, bronze or even gold. As her fingers brushed past scroll after scroll, she felt a growing frustration until one small scroll with a wooden cap twitched as her finger touched it. She brushed it again with the same effect. Trembling with excitement she hurried down the stairs to the table where she took a pair of white cotton gloves from the little box, slid them on and rolled out the map. Using a few items from her pack, she weighed down the edges and surveyed the document.

There, in the centre of the map, was a drawing clearly showing the Abbey. This was it! Hazel had very little idea what all the markings meant but she quickly tried to copy down as much as she could on a scrap of paper. If she had learned anything from tsunamis, Weevers and lizard-lions, it was that you never knew how much time you had in Nether.

As Hazel hurried to copy down as much as she could, she began to notice that the light in the chamber was growing darker. Given that there was no night, day or rain in Nether, this struck her as peculiar and she looked up. High above, the windows in the domed ceiling revealed a sizeable black cloud.

Though it seemed odd, Hazel returned to her work. When the room grew even dimmer, she looked up again. This time she could clearly see that the cloud was, in fact, a swarm of birds, huge and black moving back and forth across the sky. The swarm appeared to fly up and away but then it turned and began to dive toward the dome.

Becoming alarmed, Hazel began to roll up the scroll but the birds had already reached the window, shattering the glass as they plunged down toward her. Hazel dived for the floor under the table to avoid both the shower of glass and the storm of birds.

She looked toward the lift and wondered if she could make it inside. The birds swarmed above and Hazel peaked out from under the table to see a few grasp the scroll in their talons and fly upward. The capture of the map seemed to have distracted them for the moment, so Hazel took the opportunity to scamper across the floor towards the lift – only to realise that without Dr. Seddik she had no way to call for it.

Hazel glanced back at the birds. Scroll in their talons, they passed through the broken window high above; a flash of green light tore through the air and a tremendous cry assaulted her ears. The bodies of a number of birds tumbled, smoking, to the floor. The scroll, beginning to flame, fell to the floor after them. Hazel lunged back across the room to grab the scroll and, not thinking, stamped the flames under her hand. She cried out from the heat but succeeded in preventing the scroll from burning up. Looking up, Hazel could see the flock pull back together and loop about in the sky, tearing down toward the dome once again. Knowing the scroll was in her hands, the birds could only be after one thing. Her!

Hazel raced along the passage behind the lift where narrow stairs emerged. She fled down as fast as her feet would carry her. The stairs wrapped around the tower in a dizzying spiral. By the time she had wrapped eight times, she heard the cry of birds behind her. By the twelfth, a number of her pursuers reached her and began to grab at her hair, clothes and bags. Hazel wished Newton could let out his cry again, but the little possum remained safely inside his bag.

She felt dizzy from turning around and around and she cried out as a bird raked her cheek with its feet. Compelled forward by fear, she didn't slow her pace until, at long last, she reached the bottom and shot out of the stairwell in a flurry of wings. Hazel had no idea where to go as the large open chamber seemed to afford her no protection. She ran along the shelves and passing an open stone table, Hazel grabbed a large leather folio and used it to swat at the birds. She feared the librarian would not approve but she was focused on keeping all those talons at bay. Turning once more she entered the main hall.

"Dr. Seddik!" Hazel cried.

Her lungs burned with exertion and her voice was small and cracked with panic. Hazel heard a rushing noise and glanced back to see that the full flock had reached the lower level. If they caught up to her, she would be overwhelmed.

Seeing an intricately carved door to one side of the chamber, Hazel pushed on it with all her might. The door did not give. In panic and desperation, Hazel slammed the door with both her open palms and shouted, "Open now. Damn you!" She had no idea where the curse came from nor the luminous light that spread from her palms. The light poured across the carvings, filling in each line like a molten river. When the last line was glowing white, the doors swung open and she was sucked forward in a rush of air – the doors slammed shut behind her.

"Ah, welcome Maven, so very delighted to see you once again," said a calm voice from the shadows.

"I beg your pardon, Dr. Seddik," stammered Hazel, barely containing her anger. "I've been in an awful lot of trouble out there and you did nothing to help!"

"Quite clearly, Hazel Benedict, what we have here is a simple matter of being tested, like Odysseus of Greek myth. I could not help you while affording you the opportunity to prove that you are, as I expected, a Ward Maven. I apologise if that seems insensitive."

"Would you please explain what is going on? Why are twisted and hostile creatures trying to stop me?" Hazel asked, advancing to the desk in the middle of the room.

"Do be seated," said Dr. Seddik indicating towards two chairs across from him. Hazel dropped into one but leaned eagerly toward the librarian.

"There have always been those who wish to see the Wards splinter apart, to exist freely. Your friends, the Wardens, will have told you that this involves great peril to all, and perhaps ruination. But who is to say what is right and what is wrong? Someone who seeks this outcome has sensed your potential to impact the fate of the Wards and wishes to stop you. What better place to do so than Nether, where you are alone?"

Hazel swallowed but said nothing.

"If you follow the map you located in the archives, you will be able to find Westminster Abbey. There you must find the key to opening the door. This is the chance to open a connection to the Wards, the only chance, and it can only be achieved by you. You should know, however, that your friends must have also secured an Obcasix in their Ward and installed it in its cradle in order for your efforts to succeed." Dr. Seddik looked at Hazel and then added, "Quite a pickle!"

Hazel's mind whirled at the understatement and she thought back to their mission in the Wards. If it was the Obcasix they sought with Anika, had the boys gone on to find her? Did they have the Obcasix? Did they know where it went?

"But…" Hazel began.

"This may seem troubling and somewhat hopeless, but it is the path you must take," said Dr. Seddik.

At this, a small chiming noise came from a device on the librarian's desk. Inside a small glass dome, an intricate framework of brass wheels, levers and springs had begun to whir. It was quite beautiful and Hazel's attention was drawn to it, watching as the parts seemed to dance and spin about one another.

"Alas, our time is drawing to an end. A temporal influx event is approaching. You must not be within the library when it does."

"An influx temporary what?" Hazel asked nervously.

"Ha ha," laughed Dr. Seddik in his melodic manner. "I believe you may have heard of them as tsunamis."

"But I'm not ready – I have so many questions," Hazel cried.

"Hazel, I have the information of many worlds around me, but there are some questions only you can answer. You must go!"

As they reached the main entrance, Hazel put her hand on Dr. Seddik's arm.

"I hope you believe me when I say that I did not cause this damage, though it may be my fault." She held out her hand and passed the charred map to Dr. Seddik.

"You have followed library protocol. How wonderfully unexpected," he smiled.

Hazel shrugged. "Dr. Seddik, there isn't a single thing I understand about my life since leaving England. Less than a fortnight ago I thought there was one world at war. Now I am in the middle of a crisis between worlds with evil and monsters in different forms and perhaps the end of many universes. At least following rules in a library is something I know how to do!" Hazel smiled a thin, sad smile.

Dr. Seddik chuckled and took the scroll. "Dear me, the birds have greatly increased my workload for this century!"

Dr. Seddik pressed the parchment between his hands for a long moment and then handed it back to Hazel. "I think you will wish to have this – your fine notes may not quite do the trick."

"But the rules..." Hazel began to protest.

Dr. Seddik held up a graceful hand again. "The rules are important, but I am the fellow here who can lift them!" He swept his arm out in front of him gesturing toward the main hall. They walked hurriedly between the towering stacks of untapped knowledge and out of the front door.

Hazel looked out at the vast desert that lay around the Library of Alexandria and blew out a heavy breath. This was going to be a long walk.

TWENTY

"**D**ays and days I am working. I came closer and closer. In one moment you and your friend have made ruin of all this work," Anika ranted as she prodded Joe back against the wall with a long, white finger.

"Well we…" started Joe in defence.

"You ruined all I am doing, but this is only the start. Now we are in this haven and we are surrounded by Skinths, this is a not good situation," Anika continued waving her hands wildly to emphasise their predicament.

"I wouldn't have ruined things if you had talked to me!" Joe countered, sounding more hurt than angry.

Bec, unable to avert his eyes from Anika's face, murmured, "But we're safe here, aren't we?" He regretted speaking almost instantly. Anika whirled on him and approached with ice-blue eyes ablaze.

"Do you understand nothing, little English boy? That

woman, that thing, at Bowling Green, that was Eris. She sent them after us and will soon understand that they have not yet killed us. She will come. We are not safe here."

"What?" gasped Joe. "The goddess back there, she's the evil trying to collapse the Wards!"

"Fool! You think evil cannot wear a pretty face? Typical!" Anika growled.

"Wait, how is Eris even here?" Bec asked. "I mean, she's a grownup, I thought she couldn't go through the Wards!"

"She is more powerful than anyone thought! There is a great deal the Wardens got wrong," Anika answered and then added, "Why are you here?"

"We came to find you, sunshine!" smiled Joe. "And we need to get the Obcasix in place, it's causing a lot of instability."

"And it's putting my partner at risk," Bec added, regaining some composure. He was still stunned by this beautiful girl, but he was not too keen on being called a 'little English boy'.

"You left," accused Joe. "You didn't tell me where you were going. You had the pamphlets, you have the Obcasix, we thought... I thought... maybe you might have..." He trailed off not sure how to tell her his fears.

"What is it you thought?" Anika asked, but with slightly less anger in her tone than before. "You thought I was betraying the Rangers, that I was joining Eris?"

"You kept talking about how unfair the Wards were!" Joe responded defensively.

Anika turned her back to the boys and pressed her fingertips into her temples. She took a few deep breaths and when she turned back the fire was gone from her eyes.

"Yes, I had those thoughts. What the Wardens have been doing, what we have been doing has not helped keep our world safe, has it? I did, yes, I did wonder if another way might be better."

Joe and Bec exchanged glances. Joe thought he would be horrified when confronted with the reality that his partner was going to the other side but he wasn't, he understood. He still didn't know much about the Wards, but it was clear so far that there wasn't one that got it right; he knew why she was tempted.

"Hey, it's OK. I get it." Joe went to Anika and patted her on the back awkwardly.

"I was not going to join though," Anika added quickly. "I decided that all the running around with Obcasix was a waste of time when we could infiltrate the Society, destroy it from within."

"Then you should have told me!" Joe complained.

"I think not!" Anika retorted. "You with your rules!"

Bec swung his head, mouth agape, to stare at Joe. Rules? As much as he wanted to hear more about this whole new Joe, he interrupted, "Please excuse me, but I really do think we need to get going. You said we wouldn't want to be here when Eris finishes her speech at Bowling Green."

Anika gave Bec an appraising look. "Yes we must go, but how? The Skinths won't have moved on yet, they will still perceive that we are near."

Bec was feeling uncomfortable. Ever since he arrived at Fairwarren, his sense of himself was upside down. He had always been confident in his intellect and was usually ready with an idea, or at least thorough research. But the Wards had confused him and he had felt dependent on Hazel, and then on Joe. Joe was all confidence, swagger and American bravado and he felt just like the little English schoolboy Anika had called him. It was worse now because Anika had shaken him with her beauty and made him nervous. But he was determined not to be some sort of useless extra needing coddling from the others.

Bec looked around the haven, it wasn't much compared to the cosy room at the zoo and it was significantly more cluttered, like an old shed at the bottom of a garden. As his eyes cast over the odd collection of broken and forgotten items an idea started to form. He began to gather items into a pail in the centre of the room while Anika looked on sceptically and Joe paced nervously by the door.

After a long moment Anika spoke up, "We must be moving. Now! Is there an idea here?"

"Well, all right, here's what I have. This is a bomb," Bec began matter-of-factly, gesticulating at his assembly.

Joe's head whipped around and he focused on the pail. It was the one he had used to crunch the Skinth. It was stuffed with rags and emitted a vague smell of automobile.

"Um, your lordship…" he began but Bec stopped him.

"I don't really have time to explain. I'm pretty sure this wouldn't stop Eris and I'm not even sure it will kill a Skinth, but I do know that it will make a lot of smoke. If I create enough of a distraction, we should be able to slip out and into the crowds. Anika, do you know where the nearest train station is?" he asked.

Anika nodded. "Fulton Street. It is just a block to the north."

"Right, so I'll open the door and toss this out. You two stay back but wrap some cloth over your faces; the smoke won't be nice. It should explode and the Skinths will be momentarily frightened away and the smoke should obscure our exit. Then, well, I guess we run like the dickens until we are surrounded by regular people and race to the train."

The others stood silently staring at the pail so finally Bec spoke up again, "Look, it probably isn't ideal but it's a plan so unless you have another, I suggest we go."

"How do you know the Skinth will run away?" Joe asked, still very much troubled by the insect legs and wings he couldn't erase from his mind.

"I certainly can't be sure as I have never seen one before, have I?" Bec protested. "But I do know something about insects and that is that they don't tolerate fire. Now these things aren't exactly garden beetles and they're probably reptile-insect hybrids bred from evil in another dimension but it's what I've got!" His voice had grown ever louder as he spoke and he was virtually shrieking by the end.

Anika and Joe both nodded nervously, again looking warily at the bucket. Bec patted his pocket and pulled out the lighter; he gave it a flick to test it and said, "On the count of three."

"Three, two… one," he said and then threw open the door. There was a flash of movement outside. Without looking at what it was, and praying it wasn't commuters hurrying past, he tossed the bucket out the door as far as he could. There was a worrying silence after the clang of the bucket hitting the pavement rang out. Bec's heart sank but then an enormous bang rocked the shed and a burst of flame licked through the door and Bec staggered back.

"Now!" he yelled and dashed onto the street with Joe and Anika at his heels. Amid the billowing smoke he could briefly discern a wing and then a leg and an awful screeching noise. But he did not stop to assess the damage. He raced up the street at full speed and found that it had filled with grey-clad workers many of whom were scattering from the disturbance. The Rangers wove through the crowd trying not to move too fast so that they wouldn't stand out. The Skinths were clearly not from the Ward, as no one but the Rangers was seeing them, or at least seeing them as they really were. *Even a drab mass of people like these would react to giant snake cockroaches if they could see them*, Bec thought. Yet another thing they would need the Wardens to explain.

They pressed down the stairs and onto a train heading north. They had no idea where they were heading but were content to put as much distance between themselves and Eris and her creatures as they could.

The three stood silently in the swiftly moving train, pressed between the commuters and lost in their own thoughts. For a few minutes the train emerged from underground and ran in a tube along the side of the buildings as high up as Bec had ever been. The sights from the lofty tubes would have mesmerised him at any other time but his mind was still buzzing from their narrow escape.

Soon after, the train dipped underground again and came to stop at a station. Anika grabbed the others' sleeves and gestured that they should get off. The sign read 'Park Station' and Bec was relieved to think they might get a break from all the buildings. Joe also seemed excited and took the stairs out of the subway two at a time. He loved Central

Park, which had always been a refuge from the grit of his Brooklyn life. He didn't get there much but when he could find five cents, or jumped the turnstile, he would go and imagine himself in the wilderness. The Central Park trees were as wild as he had seen until he was taken to Fairwarren.

Anika grabbed his shoulder and brought him back to the present. He looked around at the park and gasped. Here and there the grass was interrupted by soaring cylindrical glass towers. The grass, stones and trees he knew were there, but part of the park had been captured inside the lower floors of the towers creating terrariums with hundreds of floors stacked above.

"Let us get away from the train," Anika said and walked onto the grass, which formed a green river between the towers. She found a bench under a wide tree and sat rubbing her temples.

"That was something back there!" Joe declared, smacking Bec on the back. He began to pull off his now-sooty custodian's jumpsuit as he continued. "Mr. Pyrotechnics! Kind of feel like you might have mentioned you were a bomb maker!"

"Never quite came up in conversation, did it?" replied Bec defensively, but he was rather pleased with the compliment and even more pleased with the far less hostile look he got from Anika. He turned and began to take off his own disguise with a small smile on his lips as he explained. "Fenton, our groundskeeper, joined the home guard. He took the job a bit too seriously. Started building booby traps and bombs and thought he was going to take on the entire Nazi army and save Derbyshire. Bloke was lucky to have made it to 1940 with all his fingers. Well, I really did like him and I hung about a bit. Was rather more interesting than the drivel I was studying." Bec, suddenly felt self-conscious about this speech, adding quietly, "I picked up a few things is all."

"Tremendous," replied Joe with another slap on the back, "flipping, tremendous!"

"What now?" asked Bec looking at the other two.

"We said we would find Anika, and the Obcasix. We've found Anika. Ani, do you still have it?" Joe asked.

Anika reached into the pocket of her coat and extracted a small sack. She pulled it open and took out a metal disk. Concentric circles of multi-hued metal encircled a central disc which spun silently.

"So, we bring this back to Fairwarren and find out where there's a cradle?" Bec asked.

Anika nodded slowly though she looked troubled.

"What is it?" Joe asked.

"All of this time, all of this work and this risk, for nothing. All will continue the same. Always trying to patch and protect. Always attacked. Can we do no better?" Anika questioned, looking around at the towers with a dreamy expression.

"Ani, that wasn't the mission. We weren't meant to infiltrate the Grey Rangers. The Wardens would have told us if that was the plan," Joe soothed.

"Ach!" spat Anika. "The rules, always with the rules. What if the Wardens are wrong? They have not been into the Wards forever. Maybe they have lost sight of what it is really like out here."

Bec looked over at Joe surprised, recalling what Anika had said in the haven. He never imagined that he would hear Joe accused of being a rule follower. It now occurred to him how little he knew these people. Having your life depend on someone made you feel close and it bonded you together, but it didn't mean you knew them.

"We have to do it though – we have to get the Obcasix back in place to help Hazel," Bec stated, growing tired of all the questions, of all the fear and all the running.

"You must then explain, who is this girl and what is the problem?" Anika said, leaning back on the grass.

Bec opened his pack and pulled out three waxed packages and handed them to the others. He sat down on the grass and leaned up against the soaring glass wall of one of the towers. He thought they were beautiful, their smooth rounded sides tinted with heliotrope colours which seemed to ripple as the light danced across them. Bec took a bite of the sandwich and then, swallowing, he began to summarise what had happened in Two – how Hazel had fallen and what she had done to the Weevers.

Anika listened intently then, when Bec stopped to eat, she also opened her package and let out a little squeak of delight. "Kitty," she sighed and took a bite. "Mmmm," she moaned. Without waiting to swallow she said, "This Ward, it is full of wonders. They make giant towers and fancy tubes, but they have the most dreadful foods!" As she spoke little crumbs flew from her mouth and the boys, exchanging looks, burst out laughing sending their own crumbs into the air. Even Anika joined in the laughter and they forgot their peril for a moment.

In due course, Bec and Joe explained to Anika about the growing rifts in the Wards and how they needed the stability of all the Rangers back at Fairwarren and the Obcasix in place.

Anika listened and nodded her understanding, but she was unable to muster the energy to get up. They should get back to the theatre in midtown and through the door to the Corridor – they needed to do it without more attention from Eris and those Skinths. Anika closed her eyes and rubbed them with the back of her hands again, still trying to rid herself of the endless headache she had felt ever since she left Joe at Paddington station. When she looked up, she saw both the boys lounging in the grass and, further off, the distinct form of a slender, beautiful woman with honey hair coming down the path towards them.

TWENTY-ONE

Before she left the shade of the library's entrance, Hazel spread the remains of the map on the floor. It was painted on a soft paper that was warm and giving under her fingers making it seem almost alive. A web of faintly hued lines radiated out from a flame icon, which Hazel took to be the library. She also found a representation of the Abbey, along a green pathway. With no sun in the sky, finding the right direction to start was a challenge, but using the landmarks on the map, Hazel felt confident she had the right orientation and set out over the arid ground.

After the first ten minutes, Hazel turned back and saw what looked like a distortion of light but when it cleared, the library was gone. She guessed it was the tsunami predicted by Dr. Seddik's device, and Hazel wished she had a portable one to give her warnings. She walked on for hours across the dry, stony terrain following the green path laid out on the map. Hazel yearned for the cover of trees yet was happy for a clear line of sight in every direction.

She was lost in thought about what would come next when she noticed a growing cloud building on the horizon.

Is it a tsunami? Hazel wondered, her heartbeat quickening. But as she peered into the distance, it seemed like something travelling over the sand, rather than the land itself moving. Whatever it was, Hazel had a sense she'd rather not encounter it.

She looked around wildly. There was no protection ahead, nothing behind and she couldn't move toward the mass. She looked to the east where there seemed to be some sort of a structure or hill. Without giving it further thought, she turned off the path and headed to the east.

Hazel began to run. The air grew thick with sand, causing her to cough and choke. She covered her mouth with her arm as she ran on, the small structure growing closer. As she neared, she could make out one tiny, windowless building with a wooden door shut tight against her. Hazel reached for the latch and tried to open the door, but it stood fast. She pulled and pulled as the wall of dust gained on her, grains of sand clawing at her skin. Hazel closed her eyes and tried to summon the white light that had come to her when she had opened the door in the library. She still had no real clue what it was meant to do but could it not help push open a door again? Focus though she might, all she could summon was an itchy palm.

"Figured I'd get a superpower and then not be able to use it!" she shouted in frustration into the wind. Hazel threw her weight against the door, thinking perhaps it would open inward. At last, with an angry groan, it gave way and she fell through into a small, dark room.

Hazel struggled to her feet and pushed the door shut against the wind, only then realising that with the door closed she was in utter darkness. After fumbling in her pack, she sipped some water from her canteen and felt in the shoulder bag to be sure Newton was safe. Hazel clumsily filled the little lid with water and held it down into the bag for Newton. The sound of him lapping up the liquid reached her even through the crashing of the wind outside.

"Sandstorm I think, Newton," she said.

Hazel recalled reading a letter from Edmund, her cousin who was in the Army in North Africa; he recounted winds like hurricanes that flew across the desert. He had complained that they were more dangerous than Nazis.

"I wonder what he'd think of my tsunamis!" Hazel said to the possum. She felt just a little ridiculous still talking to the little creature but the pretence of not being alone was helping to dispel the disquiet she felt at the constant sound of sand on the door and the inky darkness.

Unsure what to do next, she determined to use her stop in the hut to rest. She leaned against the warm wall and closed her eyes. But instead of sleeping, Hazel began to think about Bec and Joe. Her own adventures had been too exhausting, too non-stop, to dwell upon what had happened to them. She was sure that they had stepped through to the Corridor and so they were certainly safe and likely beginning to get over her death. She knew she was meant to be dead and the Wardens must have assured the boys that there was no way she could've survived. Even now, survival seemed unlikely or she might have to remain here forever like Crimnus – as good as dead. Hazel was grateful to be alive but there was something very lonely about living when no one was aware of you.

Then her mind turned to her family. She wondered whether they were all right; her own adventures, so odd and terrifying, had made her forget her family – left behind in a dangerous England – and her chest tightened with guilt. It would be a very long time before they would even know she was gone. What would Mrs. Withersnips and Mr. Yi tell them? Would they investigate? With the war on, it could be years before they could leave England – if indeed they ever could again. Deep inside, Hazel knew that they would likely give up pretty quickly; it was not that they didn't care, but their other concerns were too immense. She'd be a memory before long.

Eventually, Hazel fell into a troubled sleep and only woke, slumped against the wall, when she no longer heard the tap of sand outside. She inched along the wall until she felt the door frame and then the handle. She pulled it but almost immediately felt a strong pressure and the sting of sand hitting her hand. She barely managed to push it closed. What was more terrifying was that when she had cracked the door, no light came in with the sand, not even a small glow of the sky above. In that moment, Hazel knew the sand wasn't blowing in, it was pressing in.

She tried to contain her panic as she pressed her back against the door. Her mind reeled. If they stayed in the room, she and Newton would no doubt suffocate. How long would that take, she wondered? She had no idea how long it took a person to use up the oxygen in a small room. She didn't even know for certain how long she had been in there already.

Hazel took a deep, shuddering breath and wiped a tear from her eye. She set out around the room, her hands outstretched, hoping to find another door or window that was perhaps not buried. When she crossed the middle of the room her shoe made a hollow sound against the floor.

"I think the floor is different here!" cried Hazel, not knowing exactly what she was hoping for. She got on her hands and knees and felt around on the earthen floor, confirming that there was a square of wood embedded there. Exploring more carefully across the wood, she located a small hole on one side. Pushing two fingers through the hole, Hazel pulled and felt the wood shift and lift a little. With effort, she was able to flip open what seemed to be a trap door.

A burst of dank, musty air escaped from below.

Hazel lay down on the floor and ran her hands along the wall of the shaft below. The hole, about the size of a well, was lined with cool stone, damp to the touch. On one side she felt a few wooden posts jutting out from the stone wall. Leaning further out over the inky pit, Hazel ran her hand along the wall as far down as she could reach. She felt a further post lower down and determined that they formed a kind of ladder.

"Oh dear. I don't think there is any choice but to go down," Hazel said.

Once again, she tried to pull all of her focus to the light inside of her. And once again, she achieved nothing. Hazel wondered what the point was of these strange abilities. She seemed to have just a few skills and she couldn't even control those. *Ward Maven, what a joke!* Right now she would be delighted to have torch power or night vision instead.

She swung around until her feet touched wood and began to lower herself. She felt cool air from below and willed herself to think of neither the potential height nor what might be lurking in the cool dark below.

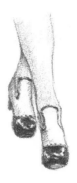

TWENTY-TWO

"**W**e need to run," cried Anika, jumping to her feet.

Joe and Bec reacted slowly. They had both grown comfortable on the cool grass.

"Now!" Anika growled and the boys launched to their feet. At that moment, they both saw the approaching woman. Just a few hours before they had both admired her striking beauty but now all they could see was the monster. They swivelled their heads around looking for Skinths and Weevers, but so far the confident stride of the blond woman was enough to send waves of fear through each.

"Where do we go?" panted Bec as they moved away down the path.

"Anywhere!" Joe responded. "There will be another subway stop further north through the park, but I have no idea where with all these towers in the way. I can't recognise anything."

Suddenly a deep velvety voice whispered in their ears. At least it sounded like the voice was in their ears but it might have been all around them, in the air and the trees and the grass.

"Don't be foolish," the voice from Bowling Green purred. It was neither exactly male nor female and though it was beautifully pitched and balanced, it made their skin crawl.

"There is simply nowhere you can run. If you are under the impression that I am hampered by these legs, and these heels, you are very much mistaken." With that, Eris appeared ahead of them on the path along which they were running. She smiled a broad and winning smile, setting perfect white teeth against crimson lips. They all pivoted and sprang between two of the towers, circling around back toward the subway entrance.

Again, she appeared in front of them. This time, Anika put her hand out to stop the boys from running. In a quavering voice, which she forced to sound confident, Anika asked, "What do you want?"

"Ah, now there is a reasonable question. I had rather thought you would be the one to come to reason. You have some understanding of what I am doing, do you not, Anika Anne Dekker?"

Anika's eyes widened as she heard her name spoken aloud by this thing. "I have no sympathy for you, and I demand to know why you won't let us be." The boys looked at Anika, impressed by her force and more than a little afraid of what Eris would do.

"I require two things only. I need the Obcasix you carry, and I need one of you. I don't particularly care which one, you can choose," she said carelessly as if talking about a pastry in the window of a bakery.

"On second thought," she continued, eyes scanning the trio, "I rather like that one," she pointed a long red finger at Joe. "Pretty," she added. Then, without waiting for a response, she opened her perfect, red mouth and issued a pale curl of smoke through which they saw a white tongue dart out. Before they could move or utter a word, Joe fell violently down into a chasm that appeared suddenly in the ground beneath his feet. It was as if he had been pulled from below by powerful arms. Just as suddenly, his descent stopped and he froze in place, half in the park and half below, the air around him pulsing like ripples on a pond where a pebble has been tossed.

"Joe!" cried Bec reaching for him and trying to pull.

"I wouldn't do that Francis Beckwith," purred Eris. "I have already pulled him partway through the Wards, tug too hard and you may end up with half of him."

Bec released Joe's hands and took a step back. Anika turned to Bec and growled, "She can't have the Obcasix. We can't stabilise the Wards without it and who knows what she could do with it."

"What you say is correct in fact but off in intent. I will free the Wards, making our World stronger and shattering those parasitic splinters."

"You will kill billions, and us as well!" snapped Anika.

"And there we differ in opinion; what I will build from the remains will be glorious!" shrugged Eris. "Now, hand it over and I will take my things and go," she said, gesturing to Joe.

"What do you need him for?" Bec questioned, not as forcefully as Anika.

"Really, all these questions are tedious. I require the access a Ranger can provide. You have already seen what I can do. The Wards are easy to mould and bend but Fairwarren prevents me from achieving my goals. A small obstacle in my way and one which I will soon manage when I have what I need. Now I chose him, we've had our little chat and I am bored."

She stepped closer to Bec whose eyes spun between Joe, Anika and Eris. He felt small and weak. Bec slowly picked up the bag Joe dropped as he fell and reached in. Before Anika could stop him, he pulled out the Obcasix. His eyes darted all around and he saw what he needed. He took a step forward and bent down to place the Obcasix on the pavement, appearing to offer it to Eris. His other hand rested on the ground as if to steady himself. Instead, Bec grabbed up a stout stick from the grass. With all the force he could muster he struck the centre of the Obcasix. With a deep rushing all sound was sucked away into the broken Obcasix. Then, with even more force, a wave of air and energy burst from the shattered core. Bec felt it blow past his back and he saw Joe fly through the air – thankfully with his legs attached.

Bec's ears rang and he could hear nothing. He could see that Eris was gone and he didn't wait to wonder why – he grabbed Anika and the bags and the two ran to where Joe lay stunned on the grass. Bec shook him, afraid that he had killed his friend, but Joe stirred. He issued forth a string of curses, most of which Bec had never heard before, but the intent was clear.

"I can't even process what you've done, English, but I say we hightail it out of here!" He struggled to his feet but stumbled forward. "Damnation, it feels like my legs are still somewhere else." The other two propped him between them and shuffled out of the park the way they had come. Bec stopped to pick up the charred ring that had been the Obcasix as they passed, and a lump began to rise in his throat. *What had he done?*

"Where to?" Joe asked.

"Midtown!" Bec responded. "We need to get back to the door, and back to Fairwarren. It isn't safe here. I don't know why Eris was dispelled but I don't think for a second that she's gone. There's nothing else we can do and I have to, need to, find out what I've done." Bec's voice tapered off as he began to think about the possible impact of his action. He began to think of Hazel.

TWENTY-THREE

The walls of the shaft were clammy and slippery, which was both odd and more than a little disgusting. She was in the desert; things shouldn't be moist. One rung at a time, Hazel groped her way downwards. The posts seem to spiral along the outside of the shaft, close enough to reach but just a little farther apart than she would have liked. Not knowing what was beneath, or how far she would have to go to reach the bottom, made the hair on her neck stand up. With each grope in the dark, she was afraid what her hand might find. On at least one occasion she thought she felt something brush past her legs but pretended she hadn't.

After about twenty minutes Hazel was starting to despair. She was in a land where buildings floated upside down and the ground rolled past in waves – there was no reason to assume that a shaft in Nether would ever stop. For all she knew she wasn't even really climbing down. Lost in her thoughts, Hazel reached for the next rung and caught hold. As she was about to swing her legs, a dull crack echoed through the shaft and Hazel felt the rung snap away in her hand. She groped wildly in the air trying to catch another rung, but her hand only scraped the slimy walls. For one moment she stayed up as her feet teetered on the last rung. Then she fell.

In a panic, Hazel straightened her body and reached sideways to try to say connected with the walls and, as she hoped, her hand hit a rung. She grabbed and her fingers connected but she couldn't catch hold. Next, her feet hit wood causing her to cry out in pain. The bump shifted her fall closer to the wall and she caught hold of another rung, holding on this time.

Panting heavily, she swung her feet out and found the next rung. Once again stable, she breathed deeply, trying to recover from the shock, fear and pain.

"I'm OK," she breathed, but this time the sound of her own voice echoing in the shaft just made her uneasy. She continued down until she screamed, once again, this time because her foot hit cold water.

Once the shock of the cold passed, Hazel jumped down, not caring if she'd have to swim but relieved to find the bottom not far down.

"Oh Newton, I'm sorry, are you all right?"

Hazel reached into the bag and felt Newton's small body at the bottom. He was dry and gave her fingertips a gentle nibble. Hazel moved around feeling along the walls and identified large circular openings on two sides. It seemed she was at the junction of an underground pipe or drainage system. If she followed a tunnel, she might just find another junction and be able to climb up, hopefully to somewhere not buried in sand. But before she could continue there was a shaking and tossing of her satchel. The top moved and she felt the small head of Newton popping out.

"Newton!" she exclaimed as the creature scampered up onto her hand. "You had better stay inside. If you get lost in here, I'll never find you."

Hazel had no idea if pygmy possums could swim, but Newton seemed to have no idea of going back into the bag; he scrambled up her arm and she felt his tiny paws clinging to her shoulder. Then, disconcertingly, Newton began to emit a very high-pitched chirp. The sound rang out rhythmically like a very, very small foghorn that echoed down the tunnels. It was more controlled and soothing than his scream in front of the lions. Hazel hadn't really bothered to be quiet during their descent; she was more concerned about potential bone-crushing falls than whether there was anything down here she'd rather not disturb. But now, hearing Newton's call ring down the tunnel, she became nervous. The ceaseless dark had begun to rattle her nerves, more so as Newton's cries bounced off the walls.

"Um, Newton, I wonder if it would be better not to—" started Hazel. But she was interrupted by another sound from down in the tunnels. It was the sound of countless wings clicking together in flight and Hazel thought instantly of the horrible flock of birds at the library. At the same time, she detected a glow coming from the tunnel and a stirring of air.

"Damn it!" cursed Hazel. "Damn, damn, damn!" she repeated, terror rising like bile in her throat. Her whole body felt as if it was fraying from the constant fear. Newton remained on her shoulder and continued to chirp. It was evident now that the tunnel was growing lighter with a bright yellow-white light. She could see the shape and contour of the tunnel, which was lined with yellowish brick and contained waist-deep water all along. Eager though she was to illuminate the endless blackness, the incoming rush of light and sound chilled her. Though the glow of the tunnel grew lighter and the fluttering grew louder, it was still impossible to tell what was casting the light.

Almost at once, it seemed, the junction where she stood filled with light and movement and the feeling of wings brushed her face. Newton continued to chirp but the pace and pitch changed and as it did so, the light moved upwards and the fluttering left her face. She hazarded a look up and, amazed, saw a cloud of glowing moths hovering above her, throwing her into full light.

Hazel saw the walls of the shaft above with the rungs installed in spirals up the walls, much farther apart than she had realised. She looked down and saw Newton looking up at her, his tiny black eyes shining, and he seemed to nod at her. Hazel then realised it was Newton; he had summoned the moths. Nothing at this point was unbelievable but that the tiny possum had this, among his other abilities, was wonderful beyond belief. A small part of her mind wondered why he had not been able to summon them in the hut or during her climb, but this was not a time to complain.

"Oh thank you!" she said to Newton, scratching him on his head. "They're wonderful! Can they come with us? Can they show us the way?"

Newton turned around and began his song again, this time quieter but at a more rapid pace. The moths fluttered down and for a moment Hazel was once again immersed in a cloud of wings. They flew down the tunnel, slower this time, and they hovered near the ceiling providing an even light below. Hazel began to walk beneath them along the tunnel. Wading through the waist-deep water was slow but after a quarter of an hour or so, a few small side tunnels turned off and the water level dropped. It was a relief; Hazel's feet were aching and her skin utterly pruned from the water. The jubilation at having light was slowly being replaced by a new round of doubt as she realised she had no idea where she was going nor whether she was heading towards Westminster or away. On a whim, Hazel pulled the map she had fought for in the library out of her pack. She unfolded it and held it up, using the moths to illuminate its charred face. She had hoped that in this topsy-turvy world, maybe the map would change to track her movements underground. She was disappointed.

"Whatever magic, or power, is happening around here, Newton, it never seems to be there when I need it!" Hazel sighed. "Well, except for you, little friend." Hazel gave the little animal, who was riding on her shoulder, a scratch on his head. Ahead, she began to hear the rushing of water which, for better or worse, meant another decision.

Indeed, not long after, the cloud of moths soared upwards and Hazel saw that the tunnel opened up into an enormous underground reservoir. The walls curved upwards into a giant dome, reminding her unnervingly of St. Paul's Cathedral in London. All along the sides, tunnels opened into the space creating dozens of tiny waterfalls at regular intervals all dumping into a central pool. As the moths flew upwards, the light grew dimmer and Hazel understood that she was going to have to go up. Looking around the vast chamber, she saw a narrow metal catwalk connected by steep stairs that circled the space and climbed upwards, coiling up the walls of the dome. Hazel's mouth went dry. The climb down the shaft had been frightening in her mind but without being able to see the bottom her fear of heights had been quieted and replaced with the fear of the unknown.

I can't! I can't!

She looked down the black tunnel beyond and wondered if she might just be able to continue along and find another way out. But the moths had already moved up and she had no choice but to follow – if she wasn't going to be left in darkness.

When she was small, her parents had taken her up to the dome of St. Paul's. She had loved the narrow spiral stairs and the thrill of trying to echo her voice around the dome. But just before they left, a big boy had barrelled past her, giving her a shove with his shoulder. Before she knew it, she was bent over the railing, feet off the ground, looking down at the tiny figures on the marble floor below. After, as she grew, she understood that there had been little chance she was going to fall, but the rushing feeling in her legs as she lost contact with the ground, and the sight of the floor far below, never left her. This was the first time, or really second if you counted the black shaft, that she had ever been high up since.

Hazel's legs wobbled as if made of jelly and she felt as though they might not hold her. An idea came to her, though it made her almost as uncomfortable as the sight of the coiling stairs above.

She pulled a scarf off her neck and tied it around her eyes. It was clear that there was only one way to go up and she could feel her way as well as see it. She remembered the shaft and the fear of the unknown blackness. It was bad but her body had functioned in the face of ignorance; she wasn't sure it would do the same if she could see the ground growing farther and farther away.

"Nothing for it, Newton," she said, and she tucked the possum back into the satchel.

Slowly, she felt her way along the first walkway, falling into the rhythm of the 'clang clang' of her feet. She bumped her shins painfully into the first stair but then gained her footing and climbed. Again and again she walked and climbed, walked and climbed. Somewhere inside she could guess how high she must be after all those turns but she pushed the thought back down and carried on.

At long last, her hands struck the rungs of a steep ladder and Hazel began to climb, praying that this was the end. The sharp crack of her head on wood answered her question. She shakily removed one hand from the railing and pushed up. The hatch groaned but shifted upward. Hazel pushed again as she climbed the next rung of the ladder and the hatch flipped open. Gripping the sides of the floor she pulled herself through, flopped on her back and pulled off the scarf. She caught a very brief glimpse of the pool of water at the base of the dome far, far below before the moths floated down and away and the vast space was plunged into darkness again.

The room where she lay was made up of low stone arches not far above. Between a few arches, small slits in the walls allowed light to penetrate in thin beams. Large flagstones lined the floor, some of which had carvings marked in them, but in the dim light it was impossible to make them out clearly. Hazel took a moment to check on Newton.

"Well done, Newton!" Hazel scratched his head and pulled a crust of bread from her pack. She also retrieved some figs and a piece of flatbread from Dr. Seddik. Hazel had no idea where they were or whether they were safer than they had been in the tunnels, but she took advantage of this moment of quiet to build back some energy.

She began to walk slowly through the low arched space which seemed to stretch on for quite a while. Hazel began to think it seemed familiar.

"I think we're in a crypt," she mused aloud, discerning what looked like tombs within many niches. *Figures*, she thought. She wasn't particularly spooked by tombs. If nothing else, her adventures in the Wards had taught her that the real horrors were very much alive and dead things were the least of her troubles. However, she was growing tired of the endless parade of underground spaces and was greatly relieved to find a stone spiral staircase curving up to the left. After three turns, she came to an ancient-looking wooden door. Hazel turned the handle and pulled.

Whatever she had been expecting, this was not it. Hazel was in Westminster Abbey.

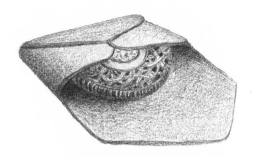

TWENTY-FOUR

J oe, Bec and Anika sat around the big table in the library. Their return from the Ward seemed like a dream. They had found the door down the alley with relative ease and passed through into the Corridor. On the other side, they walked silently along the carpeted expanse and back out into the house without exchanging a word.

Opening the doors into Fairwarren, they found Kitty perched on a small upholstered chair quietly watching the doors. She might have been there for days, or she might have known that they were on their way back – it was something they would ask her later. For now, they accepted her hugs and she lingered a long while over Anika who, for the first time since they found her, began to weep.

"Well now – I should think you could all use a good meal!" Kitty stated with a firm nod of her head.

The three children looked at one another and began to

laugh and for a moment they forgot their failure. But the mirth died away when Kitty noticed Bec's hand in which he still clutched the burnt remains of the Obcasix.

"Ah, perhaps we first need to talk?" Kitty asked.

"Good idea," responded Joe who could see the pained expression on Bec's face. He was hoping that there would be good news, that bringing Anika home would have settled things, at least somewhat. He gently steered Bec by the arm toward the library, followed by Kitty and Anika.

Kitty left them there, around the table, to fetch Mrs. Withersnips and Mr. Yi. For the first time since the park, they spoke.

"Look pal, you did what you needed to do and I am really damn happy you did. My splendid lower half was none too pleased to be stuck in another dimension!" he said with a grin and a pat on his own bottom.

Anika rolled her eyes, "Thank you for that colourful description, Joseph. The real issue is that there is no cupboard here full of spare Obcasix. We have destroyed our one hope."

"Come off it, Ani, that can't be only thing that works. We'll get our hands on another and pop it into place and Bob's your uncle," Joe replied.

"You are so naive! There isn't always an easy fix. Some things are just broken!" Anika yelled, stabbing her finger into Joe's chest.

"Give it a rest you two!" shouted Bec, pushing away from the table and raking his hair with his hands until it stood up in every direction. "I've probably killed her. You know that. We're all thinking it. The Obcasix needed to be in place to stabilise the Wards. I destroyed it and lord only knows what that blast did to the Wards and what it did to Hazel." He strode off into the shelves, stopping only when he reached the end of an aisle, and leaned his forehead against a line of cool books.

Back at the table he heard Anika say quietly to Joe, "She probably wasn't alive anyway, was she?" Bec couldn't hear Joe's response but down his dark aisle of books, Bec could almost feel the shake of Joe's head.

"Tea!" called Kitty from the library door and Bec heard the familiar rattle of her trolley. His heart was too heavy to think about food, but he fought the temptation to stay hidden in the shelves. He at least owed it to Hazel to come clean about what he had done and accept the consequences. They would probably send him home but that was nothing compared to the guilt of possibly, probably, hurting Hazel.

Bec came to the table and placed the charred Obcasix in the centre without saying a word. Kitty reached out with a cup but he shook his head. She made a quick tutting noise and came closer, placing the cup of tea and a plate of sandwiches in front of him.

"It is clear," said Mr. Yi, joining them at the table, "that you have had a very difficult time. We are most of all very pleased that Anika has returned safely, and we commend you for this great achievement."

"But—" interjected Bec, but Mr. Yi held up a finger to silence him.

"We also are clear that you have had trouble," he gestured to the Obcasix. "We must now focus on what is to be done."

Bec hung his head and was relieved when Joe took over telling about the encounter with the Skinths and with Eris in the park. The Wardens looked shocked and frightened throughout the tale.

"Just a moment," interrupted Mrs. Withersnips, "Bec expelled Eris using the Obcasix?"

"Yes!" shouted Bec. "I did. I couldn't think of anything else to do. In the journal, the one you gave us, I read that the Obcasix were unstable. There was a drawing…" Bec pulled the leather-covered book from his bag and unwound the cord. He flipped through and came to a page showing a drawing of an Obcasix with rays of light emitting from it. "It suggested a possible source of energy, maybe a shock or bolt. She was going to take Joe or kill him. I couldn't think of anything else to do."

Mr. Yi came up quietly behind the boy and rested a hand on his shoulder, "Well done lad. Very well done," he said evenly.

"But I've killed her! I've ruined any chance that Hazel had to get out of that place," Bec gasped.

"Indeed, we did tell you that the replacement of the Obcasix might be critical to her survival, if indeed she did survive the descent into Nether. However, we none of us has been there nor are we Mavens. What Hazel might do or find if she is alive is beyond our knowing. You could, and did, save Joe and struck a blow against our enemy. You have been a marvel."

Bec looked up for the first time and immediately flushed crimson at the look of admiration he saw on Anika's face.

"Isn't there anything we can do?" implored Bec, grabbing up the Obcasix. "Can't it be repaired? Is there another?"

The Wardens looked at one another with serious glances before Mrs. Withersnips spoke again.

"We will investigate and consider," said Mr. Yi. "Please," he gestured for the three to follow him from the library, "there will be dinner waiting for you in the dining room after you refresh yourselves downstairs. Unfortunately, while you have been away, the Wards have been very unstable. The house has…" he paused as if searching for the right words, "shifted." Seeing the raised eyebrows from the Rangers, he allowed a quick smile to flitter across his face and added, "More than usual. Even Kitty hasn't been able to find some of the rooms. Yours are utterly gone. We shall, of course, identify them again but that will have to wait until things are in order. Now, go on. Everything that can be done will be done and won't improve for three hungry and rather," he stopped and gave them each a slightly unpleasant look, "worse for wear, children."

When the three regrouped in the dining room, they were sullen. Despite the lovely sticky toffee pudding on offer, Bec could eat little.

"I have an idea," Anika said.

Bec looked up, eyes expectant.

"Here at Fairwarren, there is another Obcasix. It's called the Master. It's sort of the base station which the Wardens use to connect to the other Obcasix in the Wards. We could use that to stabilise things while Hazel is still out there. When we have her back, we'll figure out what to do to retrieve it." She looked back and forth between the boys.

"How on earth did you know about that?" Joe asked.

"It was in one of our lessons. One of the ones where you were reading a comic under your desk!" she snapped.

"Ah, right," Joe nodded. "Batman number 1, epic!"

"Do you think they'll let us have it?" asked Bec, a glimmer of hope kindling in his chest.

"Have what?" asked Mrs. Withersnips marching into the dining room with Mr. Yi.

The Rangers exchanged looks.

"We want the Master Obcasix," Bec spat out.

"Impossible!" Mrs. Withersnips replied.

"Why? We need to save Hazel. We need an Obcasix."

Mr. Yi drew a deep breath, "The Wards are like an intricate watch, with many moving parts, each dependent on the next to function. As you have seen, small problems in the mechanism lead to notable problems like rifts and quakes here. The Rangers are one critical part. The Obcasix are another. They are, in some ways, telegraph machines which allow us to monitor the Wards, but they are also anchors, stabilising the movements which you have been feeling. Without the Obcasix Anika carried, and you destroyed," he indicated to Bec, "we are more vulnerable and less able to understand what is happening." Mr. Yi spoke factually, without judgement, but Bec hung his head again in shame.

"But the other part, the part we have been missing for too long, is the Maven. The Maven has more power than any of us to maintain the Wards, to create lasting balance. If that person is Hazel, then she is more important than all the other parts."

Bec groaned, his head slumping onto the table.

"Understand this, Francis Beckwith, Eris cannot be allowed to access an Obcasix. She has the power to turn them into devices of destruction and they can give her access to Fairwarren as could a captive Ranger. The choice you made to save Joe and keep the Obcasix from Eris may have saved us all."

Joe gave Bec a punch in the shoulder, making Bec blush and hit him back at the same time.

"As you have recalled, Miss Dekker, we have here at Fairwarren what you might call a master key. It connects us to all the Obcasix throughout the Wards. It is not meant to leave Fairwarren and its loss would be catastrophic. We would lose the ability to monitor the Wards. We would be next to powerless."

"But you say we need Hazel above all!" snapped Anika.

"And that is why we must risk sending it out with them, to the Wards. We must do what we can to get Hazel back," Kitty said from the doorway.

"Kitty, no!" Mrs. Withersnips said, sounding startled.

"We must put our faith in the Rangers, as we have always done, Philadenia. Without an Obcasix in place and Hazel back, there is little chance of success. If they achieve this, we will figure out how to get it back."

"Exactly!" Joe said with a grin, looking like the plan had been his from the start. He held out his hand, "Where do we go?"

"This part is a bit thorny," Kitty smiled.

Joe coughed into his hand and muttered, "Just this part, eh?"

"The Obcasix needs to be placed in Westminster Abbey, in London. This Ward's London," Kitty continued.

"What?" Bec gasped. "But my family sent me away, remember? To avoid the bombs!" Even as he said it, Bec realised how foolish it was to be concerned about bombing in London. He had set fire to cockroach snakes and detonated the force of evil across universes, he couldn't be worried about a few Nazi bombs.

"Yet," said Anika, looking thoughtful and unfazed, "how will we go there? It is many, many days travel if a boat would even take us."

"What do you mean?" asked Bec. "Can't we just use the Corridor like usual?"

"Anika is right to be concerned. The Corridor exists as a passage between Wards, not as a way to travel willy-nilly around our own," Mrs. Withersnips added. "But, it can be done." She looked hard into Anika's eyes, seeing anger dancing behind the doubt. "We do not share this lightly. The temptation to use the Corridor to check on loved ones is powerful, but it is not safe. Even in this emergency we hesitate to cross within this Ward. It must, however, be attempted."

"You must get through London, place the Master Obcasix in the cradle in Westminster and then get back, right away," said Mrs. Withersnips.

"And we just wander into Westminster Abbey how?" asked Bec.

"Oh no dear, no wandering," added Kitty, "the Blitz is ongoing, London is under attack. You shall have to sneak!" she smiled as if suggesting that they were going to be just a tiny bit naughty.

"All right, let's go," Bec stood up and headed for the door.

"No pet, not you. Rangers are pairs and you must be ready for Hazel's return. Anika and Joe will go. The Corridor does not often accept more than two and the transit within a Ward is even more fickle," Kitty stated with another smile. "We can't predict the danger if three attempted it."

"But I'm from England!" Bec shouted. "I'm the one who's actually been to this London!"

"Come along now, everyone get ready. That's just how it is," Kitty tutted and hurried out of the dining room.

As the Rangers left the room, Joe tugged on Bec's elbow and leaned in. "There will be some mussing about getting things ready and the usual presentation of Kitty's food. Get to the Corridor right now, I'll cover for you." Bec's eyes widened but he nodded and as he headed toward the stairs he called out to the Wardens in a mock growl, "Fine! Goodbye."

The Wardens turned into the study with a nod to the Rangers, busy in their own preparations. Bec switched directions and hurried up the stairs, hoping the Corridor hadn't moved again.

TWENTY-FIVE

Of all the places she feared she might end up it had never occurred to her that the adventure underground would actually bring her to her destination. It was very strange to see the soaring Abbey completely devoid of people. She had visited on a few occasions with her family but there were always crowds of people touring the famous site. The space was breathtaking. After the weight and darkness of the tunnels, Hazel's heart seemed to open up at the soaring ceilings and the multicoloured rays of light pushing through the stained glass. It was like walking into a beautiful dream.

Then she focused on the problem: she needed to find a key in one of the largest churches in the world. As she began to move away from the crypt stairs, Hazel took a moment to check on Newton. "Got any other tricks up your sleeve, little one?" she asked, giving him a tickle. "Can you make keys appear?" Newton looked at her briefly and then dived back into the satchel. Hazel knew it was her imagination, but she swore the little creature had rolled his eyes at her.

The Abbey was enormous and Hazel didn't even know if the key would be in plain sight, in a box or container or even hidden in a secret compartment. She prayed it wasn't the latter. Dr. Seddik hadn't mentioned anything about that but then he didn't so much point the way as nudge her in the right direction.

She tried to remember precisely everything he had told her.

"Find Westminster, find the key and open the door," she repeated as she walked. *No, not quite*, she thought. It was, "Find Westminster and find the key to opening the door, find Westminster, find the key to opening the door," she said again, almost in a trance.

"Wait!" she gasped. He hadn't actually said to 'find a key,' but to 'find the key to opening the door.' Maybe it wasn't an actual key, rather a way to open a specific door. Perhaps she should be searching for the door instead. This was far less daunting as the Abbey didn't actually have all that many doors, maybe ten or twelve.

As Hazel approached the centre of the nave, she was caught in a web of intersecting shafts of light from the stained glass above. The colour washed over her and she felt a wonderful warmth spread over her skin. Not bothering to wonder at the warmth in the absence of sun, Hazel began to turn around in the light, enjoying the warmth on each side of her body. She began to turn a little faster, liking how the stained-glass window images began to blur together in a kaleidoscope of colour.

After some moments of spinning, she felt she no longer needed to move her feet and her body began to spin like a ballerina in a music box. Hazel began to laugh. The feeling was wonderful, almost what flying felt like in her dreams. Slowly, the blur of colour in front of her eyes began to take shape into recognisable images. First, Hazel saw the Eiffel Tower soaring over Paris, then images of Rome, then London. Around again she saw what looked like a big city with glass towers that reached the sky. On and on she saw cities and countryside that seemed at once familiar and odd. Faces swirled past too fast to see if they were people she knew. She caught a glimpse of a row of collapsed houses, rubble on the streets and the faces of wounded, frightened people. She knew the place: it was London and it had been bombed.

It's the Wards, Hazel thought, *I can see them, all of them.* As the images kept flying by, some familiar, some disturbing and some utterly fantastical, her heart began to race. Then, as if in sync with her quickening pulse, the spinning got faster and she began to panic. It was too much information, it was too fast; it was going to consume her, but she had no idea how to stop it. Her spinning grew so fast she began to feel her feet leave the floor below. What had for a moment seemed like a beautiful dance was becoming a powerful and frightening cyclone. *No, I will not lose control, I will not be ripped apart by this!* And with that one thought of resistance, she screamed, "Stop!" from the very depths of her lungs, and dropped to the floor in a crouch, slamming her palms into the ground with stinging strength. Everything stopped. The spinning stopped; the colour stopped. She stood on shaking legs and found before her a tall oak door with a large brass knob.

Tears streamed from her eyes in relief and in fear. She didn't know if this was the end but she had no more heart to think about what might happen if it wasn't. It seemed as if it would be so easy just to step through – moments away from soft beds, friends and delicious food. But how could she be sure what lay on the other side?

Hazel circled around the door once, steeling her nerves to try it. *Can't be worse than Nether, can it?* That moment of hesitation was one too many. As she rounded the door, her whole body crackled with electric energy. An enormous Weever had taken up position near the door. Hazel recoiled. Despite having attacked the mesmerising creatures twice before, her recent failure to conjure the light left her uncertain. She eased herself toward the door, clear that she was going to have to dispatch the Weever before she opened it. Hazel closed her eyes and tried to create the heat and surge she had felt twice before as she reacted to the Weever's attack. Nothing came. She began to panic. She closed her eyes again, a grain of anger rising within. Still nothing welled up with the heat and force she needed. The creature's soundless yet overwhelming song began to call out to her, painfully beautiful – it advanced.

"I know what you are!" she snarled. "I will not give in to you." Hazel said it as much to herself as to the Weever. She backed away, leading the Weever farther away from the door. Hazel continued to back away in a broad circle, slowly placing herself between the Weever and the door. Maybe it was sated and was not going to attack; she hoped more than believed. But as soon as that hope rose, the Weever seemed to vibrate and a mess of tentacles surged in her direction.

Hazel's hand shot out, the welcome blast of light gave her no warning and knocked her off her feet. The Weever's screech filled the cavernous space of the Abbey but its body did not dissolve this time. It wavered and pulsed and Hazel could see something like a crater through the middle of the silvery body. Her power must have been weaker this time, but she wasted no time wondering why. She pushed open the door. She lunged through as the Weever re-formed and surged toward her. Hazel stumbled forward and reached out for the other side, not wanting to know where she might fall if she missed this time. She felt the knob and turned as her body crashed into the door. Hazel fell, Weever right behind, onto a familiar cold stone floor.

TWENTY-SIX

The door that was needed to cross within the same Ward did not light up or make itself known in any way. The Wardens had to describe to the Rangers what to look for – a door that was undersized and understated. Perhaps something you might see on a pantry or under the stairs. After he slipped away, Bec prepared himself for a long walk down the Corridor, tapping on doors and looking for a way to identify the one. What he was not expecting was that the door he needed would be the very first one as he entered the Corridor. He would never have noticed it before as it looked like a forgettable broom closet, vertical boards painted white with a small tarnished knob worn shiny at the edges. The problem was there was nowhere to hide himself in case the Wardens escorted Joe and Anika to the Corridor – as they usually did. Bec made a decision on the spot. He knelt down and pulled the Ranger journal from his pack. He tore off a small corner of unused paper and scrawled a quick note, which he slipped into a crack between two of the boards. Then, his nerves tingling, Bec opened the door and stepped through alone.

Anika and Joe accepted the usual offering from Kitty, accompanied by a lecture about the merits of snacking, as they all made their way to the Corridor. They were trying to casually scan each direction looking for where Bec might have secreted himself, but they assumed he'd be far down the Corridor, out of sight of the double doors.

"Remember that this is our Ward, this is now. It will not be sensible for there to be two children wandering central London – least of all two foreigners. Be as quick as you can and try not to speak to anyone," Kitty explained.

Mr. Yi came forward carrying a small item folded in red felt. His face was knotted in concern as he handed the item to Anika. She folded back one corner and looked at the disk within. It had the same banded metals as the Obcasix she'd seen before but at the centre was an iridescent stone whose colours shifted so subtly it was impossible to describe. She looked up, eyes shining with questions.

"Sending this into the Wards may be the greatest risk we have ever taken," Mr. Yi said solemnly.

"No pressure," muttered Joe, scowling.

"But," continued Mr. Yi, "if you are successful in locating the cradle in Westminster Abbey, the Wards will be secure for the time being. It will essentially lock them down. Eris will not be able to exert any influence and the disturbances should cease. It will buy precious time to figure out a longer-term plan and, with luck, create the stability Hazel needs to find a path out of Nether."

As he finished, a low rumble began down the Corridor from the direction of the stairs and the floor began to vibrate, then shake.

"Go, by God, go!" shouted Mrs. Withersnips who had, until that moment, been standing silently with her hands in her cardigan pockets looking none too worried.

"Where do we put it?" shouted Joe, gesturing to the Obcasix.

"The cradle will be something which matches the shape of the core," responded Mr. Yi stumbling backwards.

"The core?" Joe replied grabbing onto the door frame for stability. But the shaking was too intense in the main part of the house. The Wardens stumbled and the din made it too loud to hear. Joe and Anika moved into the Corridor – double doors shutting behind them. They immediately saw the small white door on the left.

"Where's Bec?" growled Joe, looking down the Corridor.

"Not here!" Anika shouted slamming against the wall as another shock wave hit the Corridor. She grabbed for the knob with one hand and reached back for Joe with the other. She wrenched the door open as the Corridor began to shake wildly. As they entered, Joe saw the small note sticking from the crack and grabbed it just as Anika pulled him through.

When the Rangers emerged on the other side they were, for a moment, confused as to whether they had made it. The air was thick and grey and stung their throats. They stumbled forward in the smoke, covered their faces with their arms and tried to figure out where they were. Joe bumped, with a grunt, into the opposite wall. The light was brighter to the left and he walked down in that direction along what appeared to be a narrow residential hallway. He coughed and groped and was so disorientated that he didn't see what was in front of him until Anika grabbed the collar of his jacket just in time. Joe's foot hung over a drop where the floor had once been. The entire end of the building was missing.

"What the hell?" he cried as he stumbled backwards, tripping on the loose brick and rubble.

"Bombing," replied Anika with a cough. "With all this dust and smoke it must not have happened all that long ago, moments maybe. We should get moving."

"Are you telling me, woman, that our exit is in a half-collapsed building?" Joe barked, not at Anika but at the whole situation.

"That seems to be the case, yes," she replied clinically, in the way that made Joe crazy.

Joe reached up to rub his eyes, only then noticing that he had the small note in his hands. Finding the dust settling near the open wall he had enough light to read.

Meet you in Westminster. B

"Bastard went on ahead!" Joe exclaimed with a grin, but then he looked at the demolished opening again. "Just a few moments ago you said?" he asked with growing dread.

Anika furrowed her brow as the meaning of his question dawned on her, "No! You think he was here when…"

"Damnit!" swore Joe. "I don't know. No, I don't think so. He would have been long gone right?" Anika's face was blank, but her eyes danced with fear.

"Yes, long gone," Anika agreed with little certainty in her voice. "And Bec knows London, so he will be at the Abbey by now. We should go. Who knows how much time we have? He will be there," Anika continued with a confidence she did not feel. "He will." Joe looked at her and saw something pass across her face he hadn't seen before. Could it be tenderness?

They were jolted by a roar and tremor nearby and together they ran through the building away from the damage. They were rewarded in finding that the stair had not been destroyed. They exited onto the narrow street and immediately took note of the area. The building was a tailor's shop with a storefront painted blue. Joe pointed at it and Anika nodded. They would need to remember it to find the exit again.

The street was littered with rubble: the remains of the one side of their building and the two next to it. The wail of sirens filled the air and they could make out the grind of wheels on the rubble-filled streets not far away. They ran, instead, in the opposite direction, weaving between red-brick buildings older than Joe had ever seen. Piles of sandbags towered at the corners and many windows were boarded shut. They saw almost no one. The smoke and haze in the air made it difficult to determine the time of day but Joe guessed it was nearing dusk. The bombing was usually heaviest at night – they needed to hurry.

Joe growled about the winding streets that seemed to go nowhere. There were a few parts of lower Manhattan like this but he questioned whether this was a sensible way to build a city. After a few minutes Joe grabbed Anika's arm and pulled her to a stop.

"Look, we don't have a clue where we are going and if we keep spinning around in circles, we'll never find our way back to the exit."

Anika rolled her eyes, "How hard can it be to find? It will be quite large, won't it?" She stared into Joe's face but it was utterly blank. "Joseph?"

"OK, have a laugh if you will but what exactly is an abbey?" Joe's face darkened but he kept the look of indifference on his face.

"Really big church," Anika responded, shaking her head and moved down the street once again.

Joe did not have to wonder for long, they turned a corner and the sight he beheld was incredible. A wide street opened in front of them; it was in a shambles. Large craters pitted the pavement in at least three locations. On one side, a charred red bus with two floors rested on its nose with the rear leaning against a building. Only a narrow footpath was visible cutting through the rubble. Beyond all this destruction two splendid ornate towers loomed.

"Abbey!" exclaimed Joe knowingly and swatted Anika's shoulder with the back of his hand. She turned to glare at him and he grinned, gesturing to the Abbey.

"Brilliant," she murmured and moved ahead.

They picked their way along the empty street, relieved not to encounter any people. When they came up to the bombed bus, they heard a noise from the far side.

"Ssst," the sound repeated, "ssst."

Joe and Anika exchanged glances and moved ahead a few steps.

"Over here," growled a voice and the two took a step back. Finally, from the shadows, a very dirty and slightly bloody Bec emerged. "Get back here," he demanded brusquely, but was unable to hide his pleasure in seeing them.

They followed him behind a stack of sandbags and under the upturned bus. "What took you two so long?" Bec complained, but he got no answer, only stares, from his companions. After a prolonged silence, Anika reached over and gave him a long hug and kissed his forehead. Joe had no trouble seeing the blush rise under Bec's grime.

"What is going on?" Bec asked, his voice catching.

"Well, my sooty brother, we came out the door and found half the building had just fallen away and you were nowhere in sight!" Joe replied.

"Right, yes, the building. That was bloody unnerving. The bomb must have hit as I opened the door. Terrifying really. I ran like hell. I was afraid the door might have exploded behind me." He looked at his companions who were still staring at him as though he had come back from the dead. "Really, what took you so long? The exit is only one street from here."

"One!" exclaimed Joe, sneering at Anika as he thought of the dozen streets they must have wound through trying to get here.

"Not my fault. I haven't ever been to this London, have I?" Anika barked back.

"What are you doing under a bus, English?" Joe asked, eager to change the subject.

"Grey Rangers!" Bec whispered. "I saw them when I got up to the Abbey, just managed to dodge out of sight."

"Why on earth would they be here of all places?" Anika asked, more to herself than the boys. "There would be no reason to come here. Could they know about the location of the Obcasix?"

The three sat silently, each trying to figure out the puzzle.

"If they know, it's because Eris knows and it might have something to do with…" Anika continued.

"Hazel," Bec and Joe said together, as if exhaling.

Bec was at once hopeful and afraid. If Hazel had done something in Nether, something that alerted Eris to their next move, they had a really big problem. On the other hand, if something like that happened it meant that Hazel was alive!

Anika spoke, "We can't know it's her. Eris is very powerful; she might well know about the missing Obcasix location some other way." Seeing the look on Joe and Bec's faces, she continued more carefully, "But that is a possibility. I do not think there is anything we can do about it though. We need to continue with our mission."

Bec nodded and kicked a broken brick. He found the sensation of hope rising in his chest almost too painful to bear. Deep inside, Bec realised he had begun to mourn Hazel. Anika moved toward him and put a hand on his shoulder. She gave him a half smile and used one soft thumb to wipe a tear from his cheek. "We carry on?" It wasn't really a question.

He peeked out at the group of five young people they could see at the end of the road. "How are we going to get in? Looks like they might be trying to do the same," Joe asked, breaking the tension.

"Do you think they are looking for the Obcasix, or for us?" Bec questioned. "Maybe we can just walk on by."

"What would regular kids be doing taking a stroll around Westminster after an air raid? And you haven't got your field in check, have you?" Anika shot back, her usual impatience returning. "You are practically glowing! We can't just saunter up there."

Bec shrugged and stared at the street. It was rather annoying that he found it so hard to think when Anika was looking at him.

Joe eventually stood up. "I have an idea. Give me a minute, I'll be back." Before the other two could protest, he slipped out under the far side of the bus and back along the street from the direction they had come.

Bec and Anika sat awkwardly in the dim space. Bec had a great number of questions he should have liked to ask her about where she came from and how she started as a Ranger, but it seemed sort of inappropriate to make idle chat under these conditions. They kept an eye out for the Grey Rangers who, for the time being, seemed to have moved on. After a time they heard the crunch of feet on rubble and they hunkered down in case it wasn't Joe. It wasn't. They could see at least four men in uniforms and heavy boots walk past.

"Hit four buildings that time!" one said in a thick East End accent.

"I heard there was a hit outside the palace as well," said another.

"Bloody Krauts!" the first retorted.

"Air-raid warnings workin' though, innit?" another voice said right in front of the bus. Bec could smell cigarette smoke.

"I s'pose. Not so many killed last night as before. Couple a kids though. Why the parents not sending 'em away like they ought?"

"Dunno," responded another man. "I haven't got any, have I?"

"Nah, you'd need a wife first wouldn't you and that ain't likely," laughed the first along with his friends.

"Well ain't you a comedian?" responded the first man and they began to walk off.

"Sounds as if there are at least some children still around, maybe that will help us," Anika whispered when the men turned the corner near the Abbey. There was no commotion or conversation, so they had to assume the Grey Rangers had been scared away.

At that moment, Joe slipped back in behind them.

"OK, put these on," he said, handing each of them a bundle of dirty clothes.

"Why?" questioned Bec. "I'm already dressed. It's not like we stand out here the way we did in New York. This is my home!" he complained.

"Yeah, well, this area has just been bombed. People are in hiding or they're hurt. We can't just walk around all natty and handsome like me!" He flashed them a cheeky smile. "Also, you are going to have to do all the talking. Best if they don't see me, I don't exactly blend in if you catch my meaning." Joe wrapped a dirty cloth over more than half his face and then pulled a cap down low over the rest.

Joe then took a pile of clothes and fashioned them into a bundle. These he wrapped in a flowery apron and handed them to Anika who had placed a shawl over her shoulders.

"You carry the baby."

"What baby?" she asked.

"The one in your arms. No one wants a baby around. Baby has to get back to momma, right?" He gave Bec a knowing look and Bec began to understand the plan.

"Why must I have this baby?" Anika said, looking with distaste at the bundle.

"First of all, it's not actually a baby so it's not as if you'll have to change a nappy or anything. Second of all, the girl always carries the baby," Joe proclaimed.

"Excuse me!" Anika complained, tossing the bundle back to Joe.

Joe took a deep breath, "Look Ani, this isn't the best time to express your feminist outrage. I get it, women are the best, you can do anything. I know. Trust me, I know!" he said with emphasis. "I promise that when we're married one day, I'll stay home with our seven rug rats and you can go off and save the world, but right now we don't need to stand out any more than we already do. Bec has to pretend that he needs to get his two sisters and one wounded, but notably handsome, brother to our parents. OK?"

Anika sucked in a breath like she was preparing for a fight, but instead she just reached out and took the 'baby' back. "Married to you. You are dreaming!" she muttered in response.

"So we walk down the block, heads down. With luck we won't see anyone and we'll just quietly circle the Abbey until we find a way in. If we see a patrol, Bec will talk us past."

"And the Grey Rangers?" Anika asked.

"Well, they aren't looking for three kids and a baby either, right? Anika and I are pretty good masking our fields, and in the dusk and smoke, hopefully we can negate Bec too," Joe asserted.

Bec was growing accustomed to the constant nervous grind in his belly so without another thought, he stood up and stepped out from the bus and started down the street with his 'family' behind.

TWENTY-SEVEN

Bec, Joe and Anika moved down the street toward Westminster Abbey. They picked their way through the rubble, not having to feign looks of fear and horror. This was somehow worse than the Skinths tearing up lower Manhattan; this was their Ward, their home, and their war. This was not Eris's doing, it was their own people destroying each other. Bec thought, not for the first time, that he understood why Anika had been drawn to Eris's offers of something different.

They came up to the imposing entrance but quickly saw that the main door would be impossible to access. The huge front doors were shut and barricades had been set up all around. Bec nodded to the right and they began to circle the building, looking for a way in. He elbowed Joe and pointed ahead to a small door in an annexe ahead. Joe nodded and they moved in that direction.

"Oy there!" came a stern shout from behind. They kept moving slowly on.

"I say, oy, children!" the shout returned.

Reluctantly, the three stopped and turned in the direction of the man's voice. Joe kept his head low.

"What's all this? You can't be here," said a man in a dark uniform whom Bec recognised as an air-raid patrolman. He wasn't police, or military, but he could cause them trouble.

"S-sorry sir," Bec stuttered, "we're just trying to get home."

"Don't you know the rules? There's been bombing, you can't just amble along," he complained. "I'll take you to a shelter."

"Oh please sir, our mum sent us along to auntie's last night in Tufton Street. Thought we'd be better off there, but it took a hit. My brother had an injury and the baby isn't doing too well away from Mum. We want to go to a shelter, but we need to get to Mum. I don't know if Rosie will make it long without Mum's milk." Bec let a tear fall down his cheek and thought how proud Hazel would be at his fabrication. The tears weren't hard to find though, he'd felt like crying for what seemed like weeks. "We promised. We promised Auntie we'd get right back home as soon as we could. It will be all right, won't it, sir? The Gerries won't bomb again so soon."

The patrolman frowned but he seemed eager to move along with his duties.

"Where do you live then?" he asked with a little more sympathy.

Bec let the city map dance through his mind. Hazel was the one who was good with directions but at least this was a place he knew.

"Just down on Rupert Street, no more than a mile, I should say. If we keep on, we'll be there for tea," Bec said, picking a street he remembered near the theatres.

The patrolman looked sceptical but he clearly had other things he'd prefer to be doing, like having his own tea, Bec guessed.

"Your mum should have had you evacuated... still should." The patrolman seemed to think that a short lecture was in order.

"Needs the help with Da gone, second infantry division," Bec replied, sounding proud. He was picturing the close-knit family he'd conjured in his head with the warm and loving father, off at war, and the hard-working mum, determined to keep the family together. A small part of him wished that really was where they were going.

"All right, get along, but no dilly-dallying and no mischief," he said, seeming to have warmed a little. "Now, how old is this little one?" He took a step toward Anika and the 'baby'.

Joe's eyes widened under his hood and then he let out a low moan.

"Ernest sounds bad, best get along, like you said," Bec responded, putting his arm around Joe and easing him away. Anika followed patting the 'baby' on the back as they went.

"Thanks ever so much for your service!" Bec called back but Joe punched him in the ribs under the wrap.

"Don't overdo it," he growled under his breath.

They moved slowly along glancing behind at the patrolman. At long last, he turned away and they ducked behind a low wall near the doorway.

"Decent acting, English," Joe said, gently punching Bec on the shoulder. "But do I really seem like an Ernest?"

Anika pushed off her layers of filthy clothes and tossed the 'baby' bundle on the ground.

"Take it easy!" Joe scolded, picking up the rags. "That's our little Rosie!"

"Very funny, Joseph," Anika said sarcastically. "Let's get inside."

They made their way toward the small door in the cloister abutting the Abbey. Joe tried the latch, but it was locked.

"Figures," he said, looking around for another door.

"There won't be an open door just waiting for us," Anika stated, "we'll need to pick this lock; can you do it?"

"What?" exclaimed Joe in a wounded tone. "Street kid from New York, so I must know how to pick a lock!"

"Obnoxious kid who has picked at least two locks at Fairwarren that I know of!" Anika countered.

"Fine! But you never thought to ask His Lordship over here if he knows how!" Joe complained. "I mean he's the one who knows how to build a firebomb and yet I'm the hoodlum!"

"Can you or not?" Anika barked impatiently.

"Can," Joe said with resignation.

He fumbled in his pockets and pulled out a few sharp bits of metal and Anika gave Bec a knowing look. Bec could tell they'd had this fight before.

Joe messed around at the lock while the other two kept an eye out for the patrolman, the Greys, or the soldiers from before. Not seeing or hearing anything, they were more than a little surprised by a whoosh of air followed by a yelp from Anika and a clang as a knife hit the stone wall behind her head. She reached up to feel blood trickling down her cheek. Bec whipped his head around and saw, just across the courtyard, the five Grey Rangers. There was just enough light for Bec to see a nasty sneer on the face of a very large girl.

"Craps!" yelled Joe. "Since when can kids throw knives?"

"Get down," yelled Bec as he saw the girl wind up for another throw. They dived down as the knife whizzed past, too close again. Near the ground Bec looked over at Anika, "Are you all right?"

"Fine," she murmured, hand still on her face. "Just a scratch. But we better get inside!"

"Trying here," Joe spat back. "Never done it on a thousand-year-old church at dusk while being assaulted by knives, you know!"

"Actually, the biggest construction of the Abbey would have been about seven hundred years ago and the outbuildings closer to five hundred," Bec said, feeling idiotic even as the words left his mouth.

"Are you kidding right now, Oxford?" Joe replied, but he got back to work on the door, keeping as low as he could. Bec took an instant to be impressed that Joe could assign him a new nickname, even in the midst of a knife attack.

"They're moving closer!" Anika cried after peeking up over the low wall. A knife buzzed over her head a moment after she crouched down. Anika slid across the ground picking up a couple of short knives that had clattered to the floor.

"What are you going to do with those?" Bec asked, eyes opening wide.

"Oh, don't look so horrified, I am not the one who knows how to blow people up!" she snapped back.

Bec was seriously starting to regret saving them from the Skinths! "Things!" barked Bec. "I blow up things and scary creatures, not people. They're kids like us."

"No!" Anika growled, moving right up to Bec and grabbing his shirt with one hand. "Not like us!"

"I'm in," Joe said. He stayed low to the ground and pushed his way into the small building, the other two on his heels. As soon as they were inside the dark room Joe slammed the door shut and slid the bolt. Eyes adjusting in the dim room, he gestured to some chairs and together they leaned them up against the door.

"OK. That should slow them down. Still, there may be another way in so we better do what we are going to do, and quick," Joe looked expectantly at Anika.

They moved through the small building, which looked to be some sort of residence. Much of the furniture was missing and sandbags were piled all over. Clearly no one thought it was safe to reside here with the Abbey such an obvious bombing target. After trying a few doors unsuccessfully, the trio opened a small door with a peaked arch and found themselves in the Abbey. The light was dim but some colour still pierced the great stained-glass windows.

"Whoa!" Joe exclaimed. "Nice place!" He'd had basically no experience with churches. This was a place, he thought, where you might just consider believing in a god.

"May we see it, please," Bec asked Anika, trying to move on from their fight.

Anika nodded and pulled out the Master Obcasix

wrapped in felt. They all leaned in to look. The core that Mr. Yi mentioned was obvious. At the centre of the disk, a bizarre jewel glinted, its many colours seeming to swirl and move like a motor oil slick in a puddle. The jewel wasn't cut like any gem they had ever seen. This was slightly domed and formed almost a soft 'S' shape.

"Very well," Anika said, holding up the Obcasix. "That is what we are looking for, a shape that matches this," she indicated the gem. "Let's split up. Shout if you find anything or if you hear anyone getting in. If so, head back to the side door to gather." The others nodded and they fanned out.

The search seemed absurd at first; the Abbey was a field of shapes carved into stone and wood, formed in tile and woven into cloth. Most of the extra furnishings had been removed and stored for safety due to the bombing, but much that could not easily be removed remained. Joe took the left, Anika the right and Bec walked up the middle aisle. He tried to keep the double crescent shape in his mind as he scanned the end of each pew. *Why did they always seem to be searching for needles in haystacks?*

A number of pews in the rear of the nave had different patterns carved into their ends and Bec slowed to examine them. He traced his fingers along a curving figure and his heart began to beat wildly.

"Anika!" he shouted. "Anika come!"

He heard the crashing of furniture and the sound of two sets of footsteps approaching. Joe and Anika arrived at the same time, panting, and Bec pointed to the pew. Anika leaned in and brought the Obcasix into alignment with the shape. She looked up at Bec and frowned, shaking her head.

"No, curves the wrong way," she stated and moved away back toward the far wall.

Joe shrugged and moved off as well.

Bec sighed and moved along the aisle again, feeling more dejected than before. He moved toward the back and examined the large stone basin near the main doors. He was leaning in for a closer look when his feet seemed to buckle beneath him and the world screamed around him.

He lurched forward so violently, he impacted his head against the stone and fell to his knees, eyes streaming. His first thought through the pain was Skinths, whose eerie screams still plagued his mind. But it wasn't those creatures or any creature of the Wards, it was bombing. Something had struck near the Abbey or maybe part of the Abbey itself.

"Bloody hell!" Bec cursed and stumbled to his feet. It wasn't enough that a woman with interdimensional powers was trying to end this and all other worlds, did they really need Nazis?

"I have it!" Bec heard near the choir. "I have it." It was Joe.

Bec staggered unsteadily along the aisle clutching his head and feeling the warm ooze of blood through his fingers. He found Joe kneeling next to a tomb along the west wall. The trembling from the bombing had knocked a small statue out of a niche and when it fell it revealed an indentation in the shape of a double crescent.

They exchanged awed looks. "How were we ever going to find that?" Joe asked, amazed. "I mean really, just a little hint you'd think... 'Hey Rangers, the damn cradle is probably hidden behind hundred-year-old marble,' ya know?" Joe finally took a look at Bec. "What the hell happened to your head?"

"Where's Anika?" Bec asked, ignoring the question and looking around through the blood. He didn't want to waste time wondering why they found it or how unlikely that was – he wanted to focus on getting it done.

"I'm here," they heard Anika say from behind.

"And so are we," said a gruff voice.

Bec swung around, panic mixing with his pain, to see an unreasonably large boy of about sixteen loom up behind Anika. His head swam with the sudden movement and he stumbled backwards against the tomb. Three other Grey Rangers appeared out of the haze behind the first boy.

"It's just three little babies," taunted a tall red-headed girl with a deep scar across her cheek and right eye, "and one of them is already crawling on the floor." She gestured to Bec with her chin. "Crawl away, little baby, crawl!" She laughed a nasty, mocking laugh that sounded slightly insane.

"Just hand over the object," demanded the first boy in a flat, emotionless voice, "and we don't need to kill you."

"Kill us?" Bec questioned. "What the devil are you on about? You are only kids!"

"If Eris wants us to kill, we do, so don't get cocky," said the big one who stepped forward towards Anika. She hadn't moved a muscle since the Grey Rangers spoke, but the tension showed in her face and her hand was clenched around the Obcasix, knuckles white with fear. She looked pointedly at Joe and as the second one moved, she mouthed, "Catch," and hurled the Obcasix at him. Her throw was a travesty, thought Joe, as he saw the Obcasix hurl toward him, high and wide.

He jumped up and managed to tap it out of the air and as it fell, he was able to catch it with the other hand.

What happened next was too fast and too chaotic for Bec to follow clearly. Joe crashed to the floor grasping the Obcasix and then he stretched out to pass it to Bec, who had fallen back against the tomb just next to the cradle. A piercing whistle filled the air and the Abbey seemed to explode around them. The Grey Rangers launched themselves at the trio but Anika and Joe moved to block their access to Bec. The fight was nothing like Bec pictured from the cinema. Arms and legs flailed about, fists were made and thrown but few punches landed. Anika scratched the large one across the face with her ragged nails but the sensation of her nails on his skin made her reel as much as it did him. The redhead threw a punch at Joe, which landed painfully on his ear. Joe spat out a curse and threw his arms up to protect his head, letting the girl land another punch to his gut.

The two others launched themselves in Bec's direction. Unable to rise, Bec kicked out with one foot while reaching back to slam the Obcasix into the cradle. It landed off centre and didn't connect. One of the Grey Rangers caught his leg and began to shake him violently. Bec felt the Obcasix loosen in his grasp.

At that moment the sound of footsteps was heard and a large group of men appeared running down the aisle. Some wore the robes of priests while others were in the green uniforms of the home guard. Most were carrying buckets, shovels or sandbags.

"What the devil is all this?" the lead guard cried when he saw the tangled mass of teens.

When the attacking Greys turned, Bec had his chance; he turned back and repositioned the Obcasix in the cradle. At that moment the bedlam in the Abbey stilled. A wave of energy swept over them not unlike the one that banished Eris in the park, but this force froze everything in a near-silent bubble. Bec could tell that the events were still unfolding but they were happening so slowly it was like watching ice melt. The Greys looked back at him, faces twisted with anger when they saw the Obcasix in position. The adults continued to shift their attention between the teens and the spreading flames, almost frozen in indecision. And, in the very same moment, not far down the aisle, a door appeared from nowhere, freestanding in the open dust-filled space.

The door burst open and Hazel fell out.

TWENTY-EIGHT

The open door broke the momentary freeze created by the Obcasix and mayhem followed. Aching and bloodied, Bec gaped at Hazel in wonder. His heart kicked against his ribs in turmoil and he failed to grasp what he was seeing. Hazel lay on the floor with a silver cloud amassed over her head. In horror, Bec recognised it as a Weever. Hazel was here and she was alive but she was under attack.

In the moment that Bec took in this scene, another crash tore through the Abbey. Every adult switched their attention from the mess of kids on the floor to the mass of timber and rubble falling from the ceiling. They ran with their buckets to put out fires and filled the space with their shouts and directions. The strange presence of children was suddenly forgotten in their duty to protect the revered building.

The Grey Rangers seemed stunned as well. Their failure to get the Obcasix left them confused and that confusion turned to fear when they too saw the shimmering Weever. As Bec turned his clouded head in the direction of their flight, he saw a momentary clearing in the smoky, dusty air. Passing the other adults, as if invisible, the pristine slender form of a honey-haired woman in an Air Force uniform walked serenely toward Hazel and the door.

"Haze…" Bec called out, but his voice was barely a croak and could not cut through the tumult of the Abbey.

Hazel stood and backed away from the Weever. Then, she saw the woman who reached a graceful, glove-clad hand to her brow and gently tucked a stray curl of hair back into her cap. She gave Hazel a broad smile that seemed to warm her entire face.

"You are just exactly as I imagined, Hazel," she said, sounding delighted.

"You know me?" Hazel asked, confused but with a dawning sense of dread.

"Oh yes, Hazel. I do. We have a lot in common, you and I, and I'd like to talk more with you. It is such a mess here, why not come with me and we can chat."

"But…" Hazel stammered, her eyes flitting to the Weever, and then to the remaining Greys, circling around Joe and Anika.

The woman laughed, "Don't worry Hazel, it all seems much worse than it is. I can help tidy all this up. We're on the same side, you and I, you know."

"Who are you?" Hazel asked tremulously. The woman seemed to project calmness and serenity. She exuded trust and peace, almost like the siren song of the Weevers, but she was so lovely, so human. But something in Hazel's mind, something rational, was squirming. The Greys and the Weever didn't approach or try to stop the woman – could she be some sort of Warden, too powerful to be attacked?

"Eris," Bec croaked from the floor where he lay, but his voice was barely a whisper.

The woman approached the door and stood not far from Hazel; she reached out a hand and said, smile wider than ever, "Delighted to meet you."

Hazel took a step forward and raised her hand. In that moment Anika sprang forward, her body hurtling through the air like a bullet. She crashed with all her force against the woman from behind. Taken completely off-guard, the woman was knocked off her feet and she collapsed through the open doorway. As she fell, the three remaining Greys regrouped and took the chance to pounce again on Anika, Joe and Bec. The battle commenced again.

The big one set upon Anika, grabbing her from behind, and tried to haul her away. Anika reared forward and then slammed her head back into his face. He grunted and dropped her, grabbing at his nose. Bec couldn't see clearly but he could tell the boy's face was streaming with blood and he was holding his nose, which she had clearly broken. Anika did not wait to measure the damage; she reached down and grabbed a broken brick from the rubble on the floor and slammed it into the boy's head. He collapsed in a pile.

The red-headed girl was striking at Joe with endless punches. She didn't appear very skilled, but she was fast and Joe seemed reluctant to strike out with force at her.

"Fight, Joe!" shrieked Anika.

"But…" he stammered, "girl…" he was having a hard time communicating as her fists connected with his chest and stomach.

"Joseph!" Anika growled and started toward the pair.

"Aaargh," Joe grunted and he shoved the girl off him with all the energy and anger he had penned up during her assault. She flew backwards, though not as far as he would have liked. She fell into the third Grey, a wiry kid with mousy hair and a spotted chin. The two fell together.

Bec had been slumped against the tomb, dazed and aching, but he'd had enough of spectating. He launched forward from the floor at the two fallen Greys and his head made contact with the boy's chin. There was an awful crack and a cry as the boy's eyes flew open wildly, his teeth having cut into his own tongue. He stumbled away. The girl, gaining her feet, started towards Bec. The force of the blow with the boy's face had shaken Bec's already tender head and the only response he could make to her approach was to heave up the contents of his stomach all over her.

"Ugh," Joe grunted and stepped backwards on the verge of laughter. The girl responded badly. Wiping manically at her face with her sleeve, she gave her companion a last look and with a disgusted but afraid glance over at the door, she too fled.

"Interesting technique," Joe grinned but Bec fell to his knees. His head was swimming and he saw only spots in front of his eyes. He hung his head but pointed toward the door and shook his finger madly.

In the moments all of this passed, Joe and Anika had been focused on the fight and on the bits of ceiling falling over their heads. Now they both turned their attention to the unexpected door and Joe cried out, "Hazel!"

Hazel had barely a moment to register that the lovely woman had fallen through her portal and that Anika had pushed her. But the shock of the moment passed and she knew with certainty who that woman was and why Anika had attacked.

"Eris," she gasped just as a veined white tentacle curled out of the mist and locked onto her ankle. She grasped at the door frame, her muscles straining and screaming in pain and exhaustion against the pull of the thing that had been the lovely woman. The Weever now swooped in and began to envelop Hazel.

At that moment, the Rangers saw a small creature scurry out of the leather bag that had fallen by Hazel's side.

"Newton!" Joe exclaimed as the pygmy possum skittered over and landed on his arm. It emitted a high-pitched chirp that filled the Abbey as if it were a choir of young voices singing carols. Moments passed as the Weever continued wrapping its ribbon-like tendrils around Hazel, the guards continued to fight the flames from fallen rafters and Hazel struggled against the tentacle curling up from the void.

Hazel called out to the others in a choked voice, "Door! Open the door to the crypt. Over there, to the right!"

Bec heard Hazel's words and willed his clouded mind to follow what she was asking. Scarcely able to see through the spots and blood, he forced himself to his feet and stumbled in that direction, just aware enough to wonder what Hazel wanted and how she knew the layout of the Abbey so well. Bec had the sense of being in a nightmare where your legs refused to move even as some horror drew nearer. His body resisted his attempts to move and the crypt door felt impossibly far. Behind him he heard Hazel cry out in pain and frustration and he willed his feet faster along the floor, leaving a bloody trail along the cool stone. Bec reached the door and collapsed against it with his shoulder, shoving it open.

His entire body and all his senses were filled with light as a veil of softness passed over him. A bright fluttering cloud of glowing moths passed by like the wind and engulfed the Weever. The creature emitted a terrible wail, nothing like the clear note Newton had unleashed, and it began to diminish, writhing the whole time.

Stunned by this scene, Joe and Anika stood frozen until another white tentacle flashed out from Hazel's doorway and caught Anika around the throat; she gasped and fell to the floor clawing at the cold appendage with her fingers, eyes wide with fright. Joe ran to her and tried to prise the sickly white flesh from his partner's throat. It would not budge.

"Hell on earth!" he growled but then Joe let go of the tentacle and threw his arms around Hazel instead. "I have you," he whispered in her ear, "do it!" Joe braced his legs against the door frame while his arms wrapped around her. In a moment, her eyes caught his and seemed to tell him to hold tight.

Hazel, arms now free, turned back toward the mist within the door. Her head was confused and drained by the Weever but she focused as best she could. Closing her eyes, for the fourth time she felt raw power grow within her. This time Hazel was less afraid and felt more connected to the light inside. She let out an unnatural roar as the anger, fear and pain rushed out of her. Hazel spread her palms and a burst of light pulsed from her into the void. The tentacles slackened slightly and Anika was able to pull free. With one last mighty kick, Hazel loosened her leg from the tentacle's grasp and pushed the thing that had emerged from inside Eris back into the mist. Anika, still gasping for breath, slammed the door shut. Hazel struggled to her knees and then, closing her eyes, pressed her palms to the floor. With a sharp crack the door disappeared as if it had never been there.

"Well, that was a bit challenging!" said Joe collapsing to the floor.

Hazel shifted to look at him while Anika glared from a few steps away. Bec groaned from the floor by the crypt door where he had collapsed. Hazel's mind churned through all that had occurred since she left the boys: the tsunamis, the lions, the birds, the sand, the darkness, Eris. She could almost feel her mind beginning to crack. It was too unbelievable, too intense to be real. She was only thirteen!

Then, from deep inside she started to laugh. Joe's understatement found a lost store of humour and relief and set it free. The others soon followed. The fear and exhaustion turned to absurdity and they laughed uncontrollably. After a time, the hiss of smouldering rafters, the sounds of bombs in the area and the hurried efforts of the guards to control the blaze pulled them back from their laughter.

"Better get on," said Joe pointing his chin at the adults,

"before they notice a bunch of cackling loons or those Grey brutes come back."

They hurried back out the door through which they had arrived, moving the chairs out of the way and unbolting the door. They travelled across the forecourt and down the road as quickly as they could – which was not easy with Joe and Hazel supporting a barely conscious Bec. They scrambled over debris and tried not to look around, afraid to draw the attention of the many people who had begun to gather in response to the most recent bombing.

"Haze?" muttered Bec, but she shook her head to quiet him. This was not a time to talk.

They reached the building with the blue door and entered, keenly aware of the creaking and groaning that accompanied their footfall as if the building was complaining about still standing. Through the bombed end of the hallway they could see dust, lit by distant flames, sparkling in the air like stars.

"I am going to have some very strong words with the Wardens about our working conditions," pouted Joe as he coughed on the dust.

Anika rolled her eyes but her lips curled into a smile.

"Who goes first?" Joe asked as he turned the handle, looking at Hazel as he spoke.

Hazel looked through the open door and down into the mist. "You take Bec, then Anika goes and I'll make sure it's safe back here." No one questioned her, and that gave her a strangely comforting feeling. In fact, she wanted to go last only so that the others would not watch her hesitation and see her fear. After Anika went through, Hazel stepped forward and placed her hands on the door frame. It felt warm and reassuring. She had been blasting a Weever when she fell the last time; there was no reason why she should not step through with ease now. Nonetheless, her breath came quickly and her heart pounded in her chest as she moved forward. With a shudder she stepped into the mist and reached for home.

TWENTY-NINE

azel stood and stretched, her back stiff and aching. She walked over to the window and pulled back the heavy curtains. A crisp blue sky dotted with clouds stretched overhead; its deep colour filled Hazel's heart after the oppressive white of Nether. She looked out across the view. Fairwarren's long lawn, scattered with boulders and wildflowers, disappeared into the gradually thickening pine trees. Hazel smiled to herself as she considered that she had yet to step foot on that lawn or put a toe in the lake. In the short while she had come to think of Fairwarren as home, she had barely passed any time within its walls or in its grounds.

A stirring behind her made Hazel turn.

Bec had remained in bed for almost a week and Hazel left his bedside only when the Wardens forced her to lie down in her own room now and then. The first few days had been worrisome. A doctor had been called in to examine

Bec's head and there was some concern that real damage had been done, but on the second night Bec awoke able to see and speak. He had so many questions, but Hazel wasn't ready. So when he was awake, Bec did the talking. He was weak but he slowly worked through everything that had happened since she fell. Joe and Anika came in on occasion and shared in his tale but each of them seemed happiest to be quiet and still. By the end of the week, however, the Wardens wanted to talk, and they were quite insistent.

Bec remained most comfortable lying down so Hazel asked if they could gather in his room. She sat on his bed with Anika and Joe on chairs at either side. Mrs. Withersnips and Kitty sat in the armchairs by the fire while Mr. Yi, who may have never willingly sat in his life, stood by the window.

"The installation of the master Obcasix in Westminster has been a success. The instability in the Wards has stilled and we have seen no sign of Eris since your return. You have all achieved a remarkable feat and the Wards have you to thank," Mr. Yi said solemnly.

The Rangers exchanged shy smiles, each relieved that their adventures were not in vain. Joe leaned back in his chair and tossed his feet up onto Bec's bed. "I'm thinking a vacation is in order, Miami maybe. What do you say?"

Mrs. Withersnips, who had been sitting back in her chair with her eyes closed, as usual, replied, "Feet, Mr. Hunt!"

With a sigh, Joe removed his feet.

"There is work to be done. In this time of relative calm, we need to rebuild the Ranger programme and you four need extensive training." Mrs. Withersnips replied.

"That hardly seems necessary," replied Anika with a

frown. "We seem to be quite capable already."

"Indeed you do, but mastery comes both from practice and from study. And, the new recruits will need your help," Mr. Yi replied, at which Anika sucked in a breath and looked like a puffed-up mother hen.

"We must be more prepared next time," Mr. Yi explained.

"And, we will need the Master Obcasix back," Kitty said from her chair. "Soon."

"And someone will need to figure Hazel out," Mrs. Withersnips added.

"Figure me out?" Hazel exclaimed. "What on earth does that mean?"

"We haven't had a Maven for these many years. No idea what to do with you and whether you are the solution or the problem," Mrs. Withersnips said without sympathy.

"Pardon me but—" Hazel was beginning to protest but Kitty interrupted.

"What dear Philadenia is trying to say is that your presence is an unknown force within the Wards; none of us has ever met a Maven, and we'll need to figure out what it all means and what you can achieve."

"I just want everything here to be safe. It is safe, isn't it, after all that happened?" Hazel asked with pleading eyes.

"For now, it is. For now," Kitty replied.

Hazel looked at her friends and at the Wardens. The memory of Eris and the Weevers and the things she did in Nether felt distant and unreal. She and Bec, Joe and Anika were part of something big and bizarre and wonderful. Maybe she had a special role to play, or maybe she had just been lucky but they all looked at her – really saw her – and accepted her for whomever, or whatever, she was. It was perfect.

"Well, what do we do now?" Bec asked, sitting up in his bed, looking flushed and healthy, despite the bandage on his head.

"Quite obviously," replied Kitty rising and straightening her skirt, "we eat!"

HELLO READERS!

Please write a review

Did you know authors love hearing from their readers?

Please let Clay Kelly know what you thought of Beyond the Doors by leaving a short review on Amazon or your other preferred online store. It will help other readers like you find the story.

One tip for reviews: Don't give away any story secrets!

(If you are under age 13, ask a grown-up to help you)

Your parents or guardians can also join a mailing list to learn about upcoming books in the *Beyond the Doors* trilogy and other future books.

www.claykellywrites.com

ACKNOWLEDGEMENTS

About eighty years ago my mother set sail for Canada with her sister as a WWII evacuee. The journey was full of potential peril and the overseas evacuation program was cancelled soon after their voyage after a transport ship of children was lost. But her own experience in Canada was filled with wonder, adventure and a grand mansion, and was my inspiration for this book. All these years later her story has been taken from her along with so many of her memories, but I recall her words, and the adventurous spirit they described, every day. I hope she would like her namesake and the stories she inspired.

There would be no book without my husband. Thank you for getting so excited when I said I wanted to write full-time, and for every moment after. You have supported me in this effort in every definition of the word. My daughter introduced me to the world of middle-grade fantasy and without her enthusiasm for the genre I never would have tried my hand at writing it.

I thank her for her many ideas and listening to me talk about this story, over and over again, long after she moved on to more grownup genres. I humbly thank my sister, Christa Kelly, for coming on board and using her talents to turn a story into art. This book came to life with her illustrations. I love that this project turned into a shared family undertaking and I'd write many more if only to see what she will draw. The rest of my family I thank for being patient when I said I didn't want to share the drafts, and for cheering me on the whole way!

Thank you to my early readers, Lauren, Nora and Ariana, who made their way through some clumsy versions and provided both support and insight. Thanks to Tracy Lynch for reviewing the first fifty pages and teaching me what "gerund" means; I've since forgotten. I also want to acknowledge an exceptional manuscript assessor, Pippa Goodheart, whose input gave the original somewhat bloated tale new life! Thanks to Jericho Writers for being my port of call for so many questions. Thank you to Erin Niumata and her team who generously gave me the first professional feedback on this story and to Michele O'Neill who made the introduction, proving to me that networking really can work. Thanks to Kate Norberg whose priceless technical and artistic skills helped translate the illustrations from paper to publisher.

Finally, thanks to all those friends who didn't laugh when I said I was trying my hand at writing in mid-life and who championed writing as a worthy career. I think of you every time I wonder whether this was a good idea. I think it was, I hope you do too.

ABOUT CLAY

This book, and the following two books of the trilogy, were in no way made possible by Clay's dog. Her insistence that hands were made for scratching and not typing, her frustrating inability to open the garden door by herself and her daily walks through beautiful fields and forests have set Clay back more hours than she can count. It seems a wonder that Clay's family chose to get their first-ever pet right as she chose to work from home. What is more, Clay has, against her will, turned into a person who would write about their dog in their author bio. But this life change is consistent with her notion that the world is a weird and wonderful place! Who knew that a person who used to wear a hard hat and worry about infrastructure budgets and whose writing credentials amounted to some "really great emails" and some well-crafted budget proposals could turn her hand to fiction for kids? *Beyond the Doors* is Clay's first novel. There are more to come, which Clay hopes will only get better – after all dogs get lazier as they age, right?

Made in the USA
Las Vegas, NV
10 November 2021

34105688R00151